In Memoriam

She survived the Assyrian massacre and
bequeathed to her two children
courage and strength.
Mrs. Asly Moorhatzh David
1905-1993

The Infidels

Joe David

Books for All Times, Inc.
www.bfat.com

Copyright © 2015 by Joe David

Second Edition

The characters described in this novel are imaginary and any similarity with real people is purely coincidental.

First published in the United Kingdom in 2014
by Thames River Press

Print ISBN: 978-0-939360-08-6
Library of Congress Control Number: 2015914625

The Infidels is also available as an eBook
eBook ISBN: 978-0-939360-09-3

Cover photograph is from the Library of Congress, Prints and Photographs Division, Reproduction Number: LC-DIG-ggbain-27081

Books for All Times, Inc.
Post Office Box 202
Warrenton, Virginia 20188

*He who has done his best for his own
time has lived for all times.*

— Friedrich Schiller

To Randy,
I hope you enjoy
the book & share it
w/ your friends.
Best, Joe David

The Infidels

Those who cannot remember
the past are condemned to repeat it.

— George Santayana
The Life of Reason

Author's Note

My mother had miraculously survived the Assyrian massacre, but the story she shared with me was in many intimate ways incomplete. Some relevant details, which would have given special weight to her personal plight, were omitted. To fill in the gaps, I had to turn to historical reports and the memoirs of other survivors.

The atrocities and the motives described in this book are true, to the best of my knowledge, but the characters, their role and the story's timeline have been altered to suit the novel's structure. What makes this book valuable – beyond its historical integrity – is its relevance to the events unfolding today.

Joe David
October 2015

Prologue

The Great War began with two shots, one aimed at Archduke Franz Ferdinand, heir to the Hapsburg throne, and the other aimed at Sophie, his wife. The couple was on a formal visit to the Bosnian capital of Sarajevo when, on June 28, 1914, a young Serbian terrorist came up to their open motor car, aimed his gun at the royal couple and shot them. The murderer, a nationalist, passionately committed to a violent fight for an independent Serbia, had with those two shots set in motion a chain reaction.

What many thought would be just a Balkan squabble between Austria-Hungary and Serbia quickly escalated into a world war. Within weeks of the Austro-Hungarian heir's assassination, the major powers of Europe positioned themselves for a war against Austria-Hungary and its ally, Germany. Motivated by nationalism and insatiable greed, Europe plunged itself into one of the worst wars in its history.

In Constantinople, the leaders of the Ottoman Empire observed with interest what was happening in Europe and saw the events as an opportunity to rebuild their crumbling empire. By joining forces with Germany and Austria-Hungary, they hoped to reclaim former Turkish territories and drive any Christian resistance (especially that of their long-time enemy, Russia) away from their lands forever.

Isolated in Northwest Persia, separated from the Ottoman Empire by the Zagros Mountains, there existed in the Fertile Crescent, a peaceful Christian community inhabited by a mix of Armenians, Assyrians and Mohammedans. Protected in the north by the Russians and in the south by the British, the inhabitants of this ancient land lived together comfortably in harmony. For them, the Urmia Plain was a proverbial Garden of Eden, a civilized paradise on the border of Turkey. Made special by the many Christian missions from Europe and America, this prosperous oasis enjoyed the best cultural influences from the outside world.

To the Turks, this community was blasphemous, an obstacle to creating an Islamic Empire that would stretch from Turkey to India.

In a large village, owned by a wealthy Assyrian family, in the Urmia Plain, a young Christian girl awakens from her childhood innocence to witness the brutal massacre of her race. Too young to fully understand its significance, she is swept up by the mighty forces of war and taken on an emotional journey to hell that changes her life forever.

Chapter 1

The Baghdad Desert, Summer of 1915

She awoke on a bed of sand in the hot desert – a four-teen-year-old dropped in the middle of nowhere, alone, shaded from the harsh sun by a small tree. There was a glazed look of emptiness in her eyes. It was the unnatural stare of a child, numbed by grim reality, who had seen more than she could comprehend.

She looked around, startled by the harsh surroundings – a few trees and other plants, and endless sand in a featureless setting that seemed to stretch into eternity. It all looked so unfamiliar, like nothing she could remember. She tried to make sense of what she saw and uncover an explanation for what had happened to place her here in time, but she couldn't think. Horrific images of butchered people, too real to ignore and too disconnected from reality to understand, overwhelmed her, making it impossible for her to form a single thought.

Her mind had turned into a kaleidoscope of shifting images: of clergy with their eyes gauged out by knives, wandering in circles, confused, pushed aside or to the ground for men on horseback to trample or shoot; of people on the run kicking aside decapitated human heads like rubber balls as they dodged bullets and swords; and of a young girl, screaming in pain, while a rough and cruel soldier with a wild and insane look rejoiced in his lustful conquest.

She wanted to cry out and release the demons inside responsible for filling her head with such images, but she had no strength. She stared at the starchy-stiff red spot on her white dress near her left breast, as though it held an explanation of who she was and how she got here, but no explanation came. She was just someone taken from somewhere, dropped in the middle of nowhere, to be dried like animal hide, surrounded by poisonous snakes and disease-carrying insects – haunted by horrific memories.

She wondered if there was any escape from this inferno. Yet, if there were, would knowing make any difference? An overwhelming fatigue left her feeling lifeless – with barely enough energy to make even the slightest movement.

Her lips, which were parched and cracked, were painfully sore when she caressed them with her tongue. She looked about for some water to drink to put out the fire consuming her. But all she saw was brownish white sand that stretched in smooth waves of varying height all the way to the horizon and a few nearby trees and bushes, which hid deadly creatures that came out in the cool night for food.

She began to cough. Huge clots of blood came up, several lingering in her throat, nearly choking her before she was able to release them. She panicked at the sight of the thick, bloody globs that she spat on the sand.

Tears began to flow, pitiful tears, drowning her youth with sorrow. She remembered the gunshots, and a voice of a woman call to her, "Judith, come inside. Now, Judith, *right away*." This was followed by more gunshots; they were heard everywhere, from behind the parapet on the roof of the house – and from outside the great wall surrounding the house.

"Mamma, don't leave me," she cried, as the woman faded away. "Please, mamma, I need you."

She tried to lift herself up and failed. The slightest effort sent a pain through her so severe that all she could do was lie still in her bed of sand until it passed.

"Come back, mamma. I beg you," she said tearfully, as she gazed about at the ocean of sand, surrounding her. "*I'm scared.*"

Something moved nearby, almost imperceptibly. It was camouflaged by the sand. It seemed to slither like a snake. Fear gripped her. She tried to focus on it. But her eyelids were too heavy. Everything was growing blurry. She slept, but not soundly. Images returned – bloody and brutal images of women and children being flayed with the same care one might take to skin an orange.

She woke up screaming, "Mamma, I beg you. I'll be good! I promise. *Please* come back."

It was almost dark, and, with the setting sun, no longer unbearably hot. In fact, it was growing chilly, and she needed something to keep her warm. As she looked about for a cover, not more than five or six feet from her she saw almost invisible activity. Little creatures of different sizes and shapes restlessly crawled about; some were even airborne. Observing them closely, she wasn't sure if they were insects or sand carried about by the early evening breeze.

She listened, but heard nothing except silence. She listened harder, and the silence was broken by the gentle sound of insects in flight and the movement of the wind, playing capriciously with the sand.

With this growing darkness came fear – the fear of the unknown, of what awaited her in the night. She tried to calm herself. "The Lord is my shepherd," she recited, over and over again, until the words and the meaning sank deep, and she finally felt a calm settle over her. Then she heard a gentle voice from her past, "You mustn't worry, my child. You'll never be alone. I've asked the Lord to watch over you."

That evening the young girl slipped into a silent and restful sleep, comforted by the gentle voice from the past.

It was morning when she was awakened with a start by a soldier; he stooped near her, shaking her. He and his search party had come by camel and truck, to scout the area. Several other soldiers were staring down at her. They were inquiring if she were still alive. As she looked up at the fair-haired men, armed with rifles, she was overcome by a mixture of fear and hope. "Are you going to take me to my mamma?"

A smile of relief instantly broke across each man's face, as they nodded in unison.

British Hospital, Baghdad

The girl found it impossible to focus on what was happening around her. Whenever she tried to concentrate, her eyelids would involuntarily close. All she could see, when she forcefully lifted them, were blurred images distorted beyond recognition. Hovering over her, peeking through this blur, were two pairs of blue eyes.

"She's still bleeding, Doctor."

"Quickly," a man said. "To the operating room. We must operate immediately."

The anesthetic had taken control, leaving her too weak to respond. Voices rose and fell around her, some more urgent and disturbing than the others. They were the tearful voices of pain and sorrow. To the young girl on the gurney, being wheeled rapidly to the operating room, they were just meaningless sounds totally removed from her reality.

She awoke from anesthesia hungry and confused with a violent headache. When her gaze surveyed the room, she saw nothing familiar, nothing that would reveal exactly where she was. She turned her gaze inward. Perhaps she might uncover a clue in the dark labyrinth of her mind – a lingering fragment of reality that would lead her to discovery. But she was too tired to search. Her mind was a void, a *tabula rasa* with nothing, not even a fragmented image, to examine.

To her right was a wall and a nightstand which contained a pitcher and glass of water. Above the nightstand was a crucifix of Jesus and a framed verse from St. John 3:16. Without reading it, she was able to recite it by rote. The words just flowed effortlessly from her lips, as though someone else were speaking them for her. "For God so loved the world, that he gave his only begotten Son, that whosoever believeth in him should not perish, but have everlasting life."

She was startled by this spontaneous recollection. How could she remember the verse so exactly, she thought, but could forget everything else?

A white curtain separated her from her neighbor to the left. The woman on the other side of the curtain was talking to someone. Her words were clouded with grief. Although the woman tried to hold back her tears, some of them spilled out as she spoke. The girl listened, feeling an undefined terror well up within her, as she was swept along by the woman's painful story. Each word the woman uttered brought the girl closer to the center of her own terror, without ever identifying it.

"It was late at night when I was abruptly awakened," the woman was saying. "Outside I heard screaming and wailing, interrupted by gunshots. My husband jumped from the bed and climbed up the ladder. When Elijah opened the skylight and looked out, he gasped in horror. Huge flames were leaping into the air, brightening the night. Before I could grasp what was happening, he returned to my side in panic. 'Get the baby. We've got to leave. Now. Right away.'

"I didn't say anything. I just grabbed the baby and anything else I could find quickly, and we hurried into the cold night. Cries of frightened people were heard everywhere – some were begging for mercy for their children and their loved ones; others were reciting verses from the Bible before being silenced with gunshots. I didn't look back. I just kept running, as Elijah told me, into the woods, cuddling the baby close for warmth and protection.

"As I was running for safety into the darkness, I saw the village blacksmith limp towards the woods. But before he could reach the creek, he collapsed. My husband ran to him, lifted him up and started to drag him across the creek, into the dark woods. A man on horseback rode towards them and commanded them to stop. When my husband looked up, the man aimed his gun at Elijah and shattered his face with bullets; then, he shot the blacksmith several times in the chest.

"I hid behind a bush and remained there all night, cuddling my baby and weeping silently." She paused; she was breathing heavily and painfully. "It was daybreak when I was found," she continued. "He was a big man who smelled like an animal bathed in the blood of death. The minute he saw me I tried to run, but he grabbed me and yanked my baby from my arms. Alma immediately began to cry, kicking her feet and flapping her hands in protest. When I pleaded with him to release her, he merely laughed at me like a madman.

"He took my baby, my little Alma who was barely three months old, and flung her into the air – and then caught her overhead with his bayonet!" The woman paused and began to weep. "When I saw the pure evil of what he had done, the sight of my baby girl impaled lifelessly on the bayonet, I let out a cry of horror so loud that even the heavens shook. *That dreadful beast, that diseased vermin, he killed my baby girl, and he enjoyed doing it!*

"To him, it was a joke. A sadistic, perverted joke. When he was sure he had caused me as much grief as possible, he came after me."

The woman's tone unexpectedly changed and her words turned to icicles. "I didn't plan what followed," she said. "It just happened. When he threw me to the ground and began to enjoy the spoils of his victory, that's when I acted and did what I thought I could never do. My opportunity came while he was forcing my body to respond to his physical rhythm. Hatred welled up within me, which *I nurtured without guilt!* I grabbed the knife secured to his belt and began stabbing him – first in the waist, then the groin, and then in the face. I kept stabbing him repeatedly, wherever I could, until I had no strength left. I don't remember much after that. I don't even know how I made it to Baghdad. Everything else is hazy."

As the young girl listened, she remembered her own story. The pieces of her past began to come together one by one. First there was the caravan, then the gunshot, and finally *the man*. All at once she was seized by a sorrow so disturbingly profound that her entire body began to tremble. The woman's story had opened the floodgates. In one clear moment the young girl remembered everything. With one inconsolable scream that seemed to last forever, she released her painful nightmare for everyone to hear. Nurses rushed to her side in alarm. "I want my mamma," the young girl cried. *"Someone please get me my mamma?"*

The newspapers printed her picture and released the news that a "miracle had happened." The article read:

A fourteen-year-old Christian Assyrian girl has been found alive after being shot at and left to die in the desert. Her name is Judith Shamash, born August 14, 1901, in Northwest Persia, in the village of Shamash. She is the daughter of Malko Shamash, a wealthy landowner, and his wife, the former Abigail Tamras, daughter of the prominent scholar and Presbyterian minister, the Reverend Daniel Tamras.

Anyone who recognizes the girl and knows the whereabouts of her immediate family should contact the British Hospital in Baghdad.

Chapter 2

The Village of Shamash, The Urmia Plain, Spring of 1914

Odette carefully slipped the pale blue dress over Judith's head to avoid messing up her hair, while Judith watched in the mirror. The dress, which was one of her favorites, fell four inches below her knee – according to her mother, the exact length suitable for a young lady.

After buttoning up the dress on the back, Odette attached a splash of color around Judith's waist – a red silk sash, purchased for her by her grandmother in Italy; it was the same color as the silk bow, pinned to her long, straight black hair. Judith smiled, impressed by her own reflection in the mirror, as Odette fastened the gold cross necklace around her neck. *It's amazing,* Judith thought. *What a difference a bath and clean clothes make.* Suddenly she was pretty and feminine again, nothing compared to what she was earlier after wrestling with her dog, Sag, in the garden.

She began to dance. She lifted the skirt of her dress high enough to expose her legs more than Odette considered proper, and kicked the air like one of those can-can dancers in a Toulouse-Lautrec print. In the process, she almost lost her unfastened shoe.

"*Tiens-toi bien*!" Odette said, smacking her behind. "Behave yourself! You're a young lady. Not a naughty *danseuse.*"

She stopped dancing and stood rigidly straight with an exaggerated expression of propriety, as though she were a Russian princess posing haughtily for a photographer. "That's better," Odette said. "I like it better when you behave yourself like a young lady – even if it's a *silly* one."

Judith completed her little game by curtsying to her *nounou*. She placed one foot forward, bent her body at the waist, and extended her arms like a ballerina who is humbly saying thank you to an applauding audience. In this case, Odette wasn't applauding. She just rolled her eyes. Although the lady-like gesture obviously pleased Odette, the thirteen-year-old knew her nanny well enough to know that she saw it for what it was: a playful response to a reprimand. "Come," Odette said. "It's time to present you to the family."

"Not yet." She ran to her dressing table, grabbed an atomizer and sprayed herself generously with eau de cologne.

"*Assez,*" her nanny said. "You're going to smell like a rose bush."

The young girl put the atomizer down and bolted for the door. "Judith!" Odette said in her halting voice. "Have you not forgotten something?"

The girl stopped running, extended her hand and waited for Odette to take it. "*Fort bien!*" Odette said. "Now we are ready to join the others for chai."

The two left the room together, hand-in-hand.

The routine was always the same. Each mid-afternoon, family and friends would meet at the Shamash home for tea and bite-size treats – rice, pine nuts, walnuts and currants wrapped in grape leaves; spices, vegetables and meats baked in phyllo dough – all served temptingly with the latest gossip and news from Europe and America.

Judith rarely had any interest in the routine. After sampling the food, she would usually start plotting an escape. But almost always, before she could execute her plan, her mother would foil it. "Stop fidgeting, Judith. Show some respect and *listen* to our guests. You may learn something."

Judith would sigh discontentedly, causing her mother to respond immediately with a disapproving glance. Trapped, Judith would sit straight in her chair, fold her hands politely on her lap, cross her legs at the ankles, and pretend to listen to the chatty old women, while daydreaming of a million and one things she'd rather do with her time.

One thing was certain, she often told herself – when she was older, she wasn't going to be a stay-at-home mother entertaining friends and neighbors for tea every afternoon. She was going to build empires and shape destinies like those ingenious Americans and Europeans she read about in her school books. She might even become another Marie Curie. She could see it now, published in science journals for everyone to read: "Judith Shamash, *the great physicist*, today uncovered the secrets of the universe."

Such thoughts would fill her restless mind and make it possible for her to tolerate the ordeal of sitting politely in the parlor with the other guests.

Today, when she entered the parlor hand-in-hand with her nanny and surveyed the room, she saw the same old guests knitting and talking as they sat in a cluster on the provincial French chairs and sofa. The grandfather's clock on the hall was striking three. Her dog, Sag, who was lying on the antique Caucasian rug next to Judith's grandmother, immediately rose when Judith entered. Then he sat on his hind legs, wagging his tail, waiting impatiently for Judith to greet him. Although Sag was a large dog with a fierce look, like the statue of the Persian Mastiff from Persepolis, with Judith, when they were rolling around playing, the heavyweight animal was as light and gentle as a leaf.

Judith couldn't help noting, while observing her mother and grandmother next to each other, how similar the two were in appearance. Judith was often told by friends that seeing her, her mother, and grandmother together was like seeing the same person at three different stages of life – childhood, adulthood, and middle age – with suitable personalities to correspond to the age differences: the energetic child, the reserved mother, and the easy-going grandmother. Judith wondered if this was true.

Her mother, who was perched delicately on the edge of her chair, was leaning forward, sharing a few private words with Aunt Suzy. In conversation, her mother looked as elegant in her colorful spring dress as a Tsarina at a garden party. Unlike Suzy, Abigail was tall and svelte, with a figure and style suited for European fashions, which she learned to wear with chic from the American and European missionaries working in Urmia. Aunt Suzy, on the other hand, had no interest in fashion. She was a petite woman who preferred comfortable and somber-colored clothes. It suited her role, she would often say, as a nurse and the wife of a schoolmaster at the Shamash Presbyterian Mission and School.

When Judith entered the parlor in her pale blue dress holding hands with her nanny, she resembled any well-bred child (living anywhere from Lake Forest to Neuilly) arriving for midday tea with family and friends. There was world-class propriety in her behavior.

Her grandmother was the first to greet Judith. "Come, Judith," Miriam said, extending her arms. "Give your grandmother a kiss."

The young girl broke away from her *nounou* and ran to her grandmother's outstretched arms. En route she bumped into a table and shook the Italian porcelain pieces resting on it. Her mother turned towards her with annoyance.

"Judith," Abigail said. "How many times must I tell you: *don't run in the house!* Young ladies don't do that!"

Judith lowered her head, feigning shame, "I'm sorry, Mamma," she said. "I forgot."

Abigail merely shook her head. "Yes, of course," she said. "Forgive me, Judith. I forget how easily you forget things."

Judith feigned her shame just long enough to placate her mother; when it was safe, she turned her attention to her grandmother and gave her a big hug.

"How nice you smell," her grandmother said. "Is that the fragrance I bought you in Beirut?"

"Oh, yes," she said. "I just love it. I spray it on every night before I go to bed, and I pretend that I am sleeping in the gardens of Shalimar."

"I'm so pleased you like it." And she patted a chair next to her. "Here, sit next to me. Tell me what you learned today in school."

Judith excitedly told her grandmother about the *Statue de la Liberté*, the subject of today's history class. "Did you know the French gave it to America as a symbol of their friendship?" she said, proudly sharing her knowledge. "I even memorized 'The New Colossus,' just as it appears on the Statue. Want to hear it?" Before grandmother could answer, Judith jumped to her feet and began to recite it with exaggerated gestures, as though she were performing it for a large audience on a great stage in America or Europe.

"'The New Colossus' by Emma Lazarus," she said, raising her voice high enough to be heard by everyone in the room. With just those opening words, Judith was able to end the conversation in the room and become the center of attention. Stunned, Abigail merely shook her head in disbelief.

"Give me your tired, your poor," Judith said, emphasizing her words with exaggerated theatrical gestures. "Your huddled masses yearning to breathe free, the wretched refuse of your teeming shore. Send these, the homeless, tempest-tost to me," and then, for a dramatic finale, she shot her right arm straight into the air as though she were holding a torch. She stiffened like the Statue of Liberty and said commandingly: "*I lift my lamp beside the golden door!*"

"Bravo, my darling," her grandmother said, applauding. "Excellent."

The others also applauded. Judith smiled, pleased; she then curtsied to the guests and sat down next to her grandmother again. "Did I do all right, Grandmamma?"

"Absolutely," Miriam said. "You have remarkable delivery. You could be another Sarah Bernhardt."

"Was I *that* good?"

"*Better.*"

"Maybe that's what I should be when I'm older. An actress." She thought about it for a moment. "Yes, that's exactly what I'll be – another Sarah Bernhardt."

Judith's attention shifted to her grandmother's lapis lazuli stone brooch with its swirling specks of golden pyrite; this stunning blue stone, favored by ancient Mesopotamians, was framed in gold with a filigree trim, and it was pinned to her grandmother's suit jacket. Carved on the face of the stone was an ancient deity sitting on his throne with a staff in one hand and a ring in the other. Like several other pieces of her grandmother's jewelry, it was antique, which was clearly evident from the wear and design of the stone. Her husband unearthed the carved stone when he was planting flowers a few years ago. How old this piece was no one in the family knew or cared to know. One thing was certain: it was valuable, maybe even museum-worthy.

Although it wasn't unusual for neighbors and friends to discover such treasures from the past buried on their land, none of the pieces that Judith had ever seen was as beautiful and important as her grandmother's brooch. This might explain why Miriam never wore it publicly. It was in bad taste, she would often tell Judith, to flaunt wealth. It would only make those with less more envious. So she would always practice what she preached and wear her favorite pieces at home and during private social occasions with family friends.

Judith eyed the brooch, fascinated by its detail and the image it evoked of her ancient Assyrian past. "One day it'll be yours," Miriam said, "Would you like that?"

"Oh yes, Grandmamma. Very much." She then added unexpectedly, "Will it make me rich like Daddy?"

"I don't know about that," Miriam said. "But I am sure it will take good care of your financial needs, if you should ever sell it."

Abigail turned to her mother angrily. "Mother, please," Abigail snapped. "I forbid you to encourage such materialism. These are troubled times. The last thing I need is a spoiled child."

Miriam met her anger with a maternal smile. "Have you already forgotten how I spoiled you? Yet look at you, Abigail. You have grown up to become a very sensible woman. So tell me, my dear daughter, what is the harm in indulging my grandchild a little?"

"Times are changing, Mother. War is in the air. No one knows for sure what Demir Pasha will do next. I can't afford to have a daughter who isn't sensibly grounded and prepared for any eventuality."

"Oh, you modern women," Miriam said. "You worry about everything. You must learn to leave such matters to our men to sort out."

"What men?" Abigail said bitterly. "Those men who betrayed us and fled to America for a better life?"

"My dear daughter," Miriam said. "Haven't you learned from the teachings of your father yet? There are some things you just must leave in God's hands."

Judith had heard it before – whether it was coming from her father, mother or their friends. When they weren't complaining about the men who ran off to America, they were worrying about the Kurds who slipped away from their mountain villages at night to rob the Christians in the Plain. So Judith did what any other thirteen-year-old would do in such a situation – she stopped listening to the conversation and greedily inspected the tray of sweets placed on a table near her.

There was the *napeloni*, filled with white custard between layers of flaky pastry; the Persian roulette, a white cake filled with cream and topped with pista-chios; and the pastry squares dipped in honey and stuffed with walnuts. Her favorite treat, which the cook always prepared just for her, was the *kada*, a dry pastry with a butter, sugar and flour filling. The pastry was cut into small rectangles and served warm, exactly as Judith preferred.

Judith took advantage of the quick verbal exchange between her grandmother and mother to help herself generously to the *kada* placed on the table near her. Sag immediately lifted his head from its resting place on the rug and gave full attention to Judith as she greedily moved the pastry from the plate to her mouth. After she ate all she wanted, she slipped some to the dog, who grabbed it with his huge mouth.

"Judith!" her mother said, catching her in the act.

"It fell from my hands," she said, riddled with guilt. "Honest, Mamma."

Her mother wiggled a long, delicate finger at her disapprovingly. "How many times must I tell you? Don't feed the dog at the table. It will make him impossible to have around during mealtime."

"Yes, Mamma."

Abigail gazed at Judith long enough to make her point. Judith showed repentance by reaching for another piece of the *kada* and eating it in its entirety with lady-like decorum. Her mother nodded approvingly before returning her attention to the guests.

Judith grew totally uncomfortable, listening to the women discuss the latest Turkish atrocities initiated by Demir Pasha against the Christians. She suddenly wanted to escape to her room and play with her dolls. But Judith knew if she asked her mother for permission, her mother would only say no.

So she did the only thing she could do in such a situation. Without considering the consequences, Judith "accidentally" let some of the tea she was sipping from an hourglass-shaped cup spill on her favorite blue dress.

"Look what you've done!" Abigail scolded. "You've *ruined* your dress."

"But it was hot and…"

"No excuses," her mother said. "Go to your room and change immediately. And don't forget to tell Rebecca to wash it before the stain sets." Judith set the glass and saucer down on the table. Looking as though she were deeply ashamed of herself, she rose and walked slowly towards the hall, repressing an enormous urge to run happily from the room.

Chapter 3

Ministry of War, Constantinople

The Persian Governor was led straight to Demir Pasha's office at *La Sublime Porte*, without unneeded formalities or polite delays. This startled the Governor. When he entered the Minister's office, the Pasha stepped from behind his desk and walked halfway through the room to greet him, which also startled the Governor. *What could the Minister want from him that he needed to show such special courtesy?*

The Pasha provided no immediate clue. He politely extended his hand and gave the Governor a firm handshake. "*Hoş geldiniz!*" He looked the Governor straight in the eyes. "Welcome to Constantinople!"

"*Hoş bulduk!*" the Governor responded; he met the Minister's gaze and held it long enough to convey confidence, shaking Demir Pasha's hand firmly to confirm his own strength.

Gazi Demir then gestured for the Governor to sit down opposite him. He was dressed perfectly in his military uniform, with the elegance and flare expected of a lean, tightly built, high-ranking Turkish officer. On the wall facing the Governor were two portraits, one of the German Kaiser and the other of the Pasha. Both men were painted in full military uniform on horseback. On the portrait, the Pasha resembled a Turk posing as a Prussian officer, a *Hohenzollern*, right down to the enlarged handlebar mustache.

In person, the Pasha could have been mistaken for the real thing – a man of heritage, an aristocrat who had inherited his power at *La Sublime Porte* by birth. Yet the Persian Governor, who grew up in royal circles, immediately saw the Pasha for what he was. Despite his elegant façade and his recent marriage to a princess, the Pasha was in the Governor's eyes merely a gatekeeper's son, a military man who single-handedly overthrew the Sultan during a coup d'état and boldly killed his predecessor, the Minister of War, during a swift attack at *La Sublime Porte*.

While they were enjoying light conversation and chai, the Governor wondered where this meeting was heading. He felt a shade of discomfort because of the way the Minister was studying him – examining every nuance of his behavior as though he were searching for the Governor's vulnerability. The Governor was ready to cut to the point and ask the Pasha for the reason for this invitation to Constantinople when the Pasha said, quite unexpectedly, "I need your help, Sardar Jamshid."

The Governor's curiosity peaked. He immediately set his tea glass on the saucer and placed both on the table. *Finally, I am going to find out what he wants,* the Governor thought. *Why he summoned me from Urmia for a private audience with him in Constantinople.*

The Governor leaned back in his chair to hear what the Pasha had to say. Like so many impoverished aristocrats, the Governor was always looking for new ways to enrich himself. He wondered if this was the opportunity he was waiting for.

"In what way, Efendi, can I serve you?" he said respectfully. Years of deference to the Royal Family in Teheran had taught the Governor to respond to leaders with suitable humility and politeness. It strengthened their self-esteem and made them easier to manipulate.

"As you may have heard, I have great plans for Turkey," the Pasha said with what seemed to the Governor a deceptive understatement. "But before I can implement them, I will need the assistance of powerful friends like you."

"You greatly flatter me, Efendi. I am only a governor of a small piece of land in Northwest Persia. I am hardly significant enough to be of any real assistance to someone as powerful as you."

"You underestimate your importance, Governor. I need men like you to help me realize my goal."

"I am most flattered. But how can a humble servant like me ever serve you in any meaningful way?"

"I want you to help me rebuild my empire and stretch it to the East."

"You mean into Persia?"

"Further."

"India?" the Governor said, stunned by the Pasha's ambition.

"Yes, India."

The Governor had heard that the Pasha was ambitious, but he never realized how ambitious.

"What about the Russians? Aren't you worried how they'll react the minute you cross the Zagros Mountains into Persia?"

"Not at all. I will simply distract them."

"You'll need to do more than distract them if you want to enter Persia."

"That's why I need you – and your many friends."

"You are mistaken, Efendi. I don't have the kind of friends that will be of use to you."

"What about those Kurds who so generously share their plunder with you?"

The Governor was surprised that the Minister knew about his private arrangements with the Kurds. The Pasha's spies had obviously done their work. He wondered if he also knew about his dislike for Persia's Royal Family. "Those Kurds can be of no use," the Governor said. "They're just petty thieves who will retreat at the sight of the Russians. No, my friend, you will need the military strength of a great army to take on the Russians."

Demir sat perfectly erect, as though he had complete control of every muscle in his body. "Let me clarify, Sardar," he said, showing he had the same control of his thoughts as he had of every muscle in his body. "Maybe then you'll understand exactly how you can help me. First of all, I don't expect your friends to come in contact with the Russians. I will do that myself by destroying their military defenses in the north. I will do it so effectively and unexpectedly that the Russian troops in Persia will have to rush to their aid. At that point, I want your Kurdish friends to make their move – *after the Russians withdraw.* I want them to sweep down on the Plain and, with the assistance of my backup army, cleanse Persia once and for all of every last infidel."

"That's very clever," the Governor said. "But are you sure your military can achieve such a victory in the north?"

"I have total confidence in my plan," the Minister said with the air of a military man comfortable with the nuances of fighting successful wars.

Although he knew Gazi had had many remarkable military successes, which led to the Pasha's current position of power, the Governor also knew Gazi had had many embarrassing defeats. The Governor was certain – if the Pasha embarked on this plan, it would be a huge failure. Partnering with the Pasha in any way could be a foolish decision. "I don't think it would be wise to become involved," the Governor said after some thought. "Such cooperation would infuriate the Royal Family in Teheran – and I could easily be beheaded."

"First, there's no chance of that, if you are discrete. Second, if you cooperate with me, you will be beheading them."

The Governor was amused at the thought of the Royal Family being **beheaded**. What a wonderful moment of revenge it would be to eliminate them.

He remembered how swiftly he was expelled from Teheran after his cousin became the shah. The last thing his cousin wanted was to have an ambitious man like the Governor around to stir trouble. Wouldn't it be a wonderful retribution if the Pasha did conquer Persia?

"As much as your plan intrigues me, I don't see how it can ever work," the Governor said. "For one thing, many of the mountain tribes fiercely hate each other. Getting them to work together would be almost impossible."

"On the contrary," the Pasha said. "Not if you do what my governors in Turkey are doing."

"And what's that?"

"They are uniting the tribes by redirecting their hatred towards their common enemy, the Christians."

There was no question about it. The Pasha was totally mad. He was willing to risk the entire Ottoman Empire in order to follow a dream that could only lead to defeat. Was this the type of leader the Governor wanted to partner with?

"You realize," he said, "I would be asking my friends to take large risks for an uncertain outcome."

"What risks? The Christians won't retaliate. They're unarmed."

"But what if they aren't? What if the Russians armed them?"

"Then disarm them," he said. "If you will assist me in the Turkification of the Middle East, I will give you what you want when my army reaches Teheran."

"What exactly would that be?"

"The Peacock Throne."

The Governor found it laughable that the Pasha had the temerity to make such an offer, considering his circumstances. Everyone knew Turkey's treasury was depleted, and its army was exhausted from the last two Balkan wars. In fact, it was rumored that the army was so weak that it couldn't even defend itself against Persia's ragged military. To the world, the Ottoman Empire was a sick power, a has-been that was being torn apart at the fringes by every rogue nation in Europe. How could he ever dream of taking on Russia or even conquering India, the crown jewel of Great Britain, and successfully Turkify the Middle East?

"That all sounds very tempting," Sardar Jamshid said with diplomatic restraint. "But do you really have the military and financial resources to achieve such a goal?"

"What I don't have now I will have soon," Gazi said. "I am currently modernizing the military and replacing the older officers with younger ones. And for the money and training, I will seek assistance from Europe ."

The Governor was growing impatient listening to the Minister's grandiose ideas. He already knew from reliable sources that the Russians had plans in place to destroy Turkey.

They were not only working with the major powers of Europe to chip away at what was left of the Ottoman Empire, but also arming the Armenians and the Christians in the north to fight against the Turks. To the Russians, the Turks were a savage force that was obstructing access to warm water ports in the south. The Pasha's plan could never be accomplished. He would face enormous resistance from the Russians and their European allies the moment he attempted to implement it. The Governor wanted to say this to the Pasha, but he knew it would be better to remain silent.

"But who in Europe can you trust? You can't turn to the English for assistance," the Governor said. "When you needed them during the Balkan Wars, they completely ignored you by pursuing their own interests in Egypt and the Persian Gulf. Surely you don't think it will be any different this time, do you?"

"You're absolutely right," the Pasha said. "At this moment, the English are probably plotting with the Russians against us. Those uprisings in Armenia and the Balkans are not independent acts of nationalism, as some powers would like us to believe. No, I am sure they are all a part of the Christian plot to break up the Ottoman Empire into manageable pieces."

"Doesn't the same apply to the French?" the Governor continued. "All they're after is Palestine and Syria." He noted the Kaiser's portrait on horseback. Despite the Kaiser's atrophied left arm, which hung lifelessly to one side, in uniform he still resembled a formidable leader who could take on the world with one mighty arm. "That leaves one major European power – the Germans."

"Exactly, the Germans."

"Will the Kaiser cooperate?" he asked pointedly. "He isn't a fool, and he will put a high price on what he gives."

"I am prepared for that."

"Are you prepared to lose more than you will gain from him? Are you willing to give up some control of Turkey just for his financial and military assistance?"

"Let me put it another way," the Minister said. "I will do whatever I need to do to make him my friend. I will appeal to his greed, which I will feed generously. In return, I will take whatever materials, military support and money I can get from him. Never forget the Prussian military is the most sophisticated and well-trained force in the world. They alone can turn my worn-out army into one of the most dangerous war machines in Asia. With Germany as my ally, there is *nothing* I can't achieve."

"But what can you give Germany in return?" the Governor asked. "The Kaiser will want something."

"I realize that, and I'm willing to give him exactly what he wants."

"What would that be?"

"*Europe.*"

"Europe?" the Governor said, astonished. "How will you ever accomplish that?"

"With the assistance of three hundred million Muslims around the world."

"How in the name of Allah can religious radicals in Africa and Asia be useful to anyone in Europe?"

"Simple," the Pasha said. "Properly motivated, those crazed radicals can be a formidable threat to the Christians from within their colonies. All I need to do is light the fuse, and overnight the Allies will be crippled by major uprisings around the world."

"A *jihad*?" the Governor said, amused.

"Exactly. A *jihad*! It will distract the Europeans while the Kaiser conquers Europe."

The Governor immediately pictured the great Prussian Kaiser in his *pickelhaube* helmet clutching the globe with his mighty right hand as though he were going to devour it like an apple. "You know, that could work," he said, smiling.

"Then it's agreed?" the Pasha asked.

"Yes," the Governor said, "it's agreed."

"*Yavaş, yavaş*," the Pasha said. "Slowly but surely, everything is falling into place, and Turkey will rule once again."

Chapter 4

The Village of Shamash, the Urmia Plain

Most of the house reflected Abigail's traditional European taste, except for the library. This was Malko's room. On one long wall were floor-to-ceiling bookshelves with a huge selection of books on Assyrian history. Mixed with the books was an assortment of Assyrian antiquities, which included an old clay tablet in Assyrian cuneiform and an Aramaic Bible, believed to be one of the oldest in the world.

Of all Malko's antiquities, the one which he prized the most was the fifteenth-century painting of the three Apostles – St Thomas, St Bartholomew, and St Thaddeus. It was a spectacular painting that covered most of the wall, and it depicted the Apostles entering the ancient Assyrian city of Edessa, where they were being greeted by a throng of worshippers. The painting was done in the Italian Renaissance style similar to Michelangelo's; it was populated with sensual human figures in motion, each revealing a life-like and uniquely individual personality.

Malko was gazing at the painting, silently enjoying his private window into the past, when his solitude was interrupted by a burst of energy. The door flew open, as though forced by a mighty wind, and Judith rushed into the library, followed by her faithful companion, Sag. Startled, he jerked his head towards her. Though she was told many times to knock before entering, she always managed to forget. For Judith, everything was too important for it to wait, and she always had an excuse for her unmannerly behavior.

Dressed in her school-girl white dress, she was no longer the same prim thirteen-year-old she had been when she left for school earlier that day; her clothes were wrinkled and her hair was uncombed, and Sag's dark hairs were seen everywhere on the front of her dress, obviously the result of their affectionate after-school embrace.

"Daddy, Daddy," she said urgently. "Is it true? Are we *really* gods?"

Although Malko resembled a six-foot Assyrian warrior, mighty enough to terrify most men if provoked, his dainty, four-foot-tall daughter was able to reduce him to a harmless adolescent by simply charming him with her girlish presence. Whatever annoyance he might have felt at having his solitude interrupted quickly disappeared. "What are you talking about?" he asked, amused.

"Are we gods?" Judith repeated.

"Of course not," he said. "Whatever gave you that idea?"

"Well, my teacher told me Shamash was an Assyrian god. So I thought, if Shamash was an Assyrian god, that would make us gods too?" She stood before him, overflowing with girlish innocence. "After all, our name *is* Shamash."

"I hate to disappoint you, Judith, but we are definitely not gods. It is just a coincidence that we happen to have the same name as the sun god."

"Well, you better straighten out grandma," Judith said, annoyed. "She told me I was God's child."

His strong and prominent features, so uniquely characteristic of his ancient Assyrian ancestors, cracked into an affectionate smile. "Did she now?"

"She most definitely did." She cocked her head, stared straight at him, and said without lifting her gaze: "So who's correct – you or her?"

"Both of us."

"That doesn't make sense, Daddy. How can you both be right?"

"Your grandmother is talking about God the Creator, not Shamash the sun god. In that sense, we are all God's children. But you can be assured that does not make us gods."

"Then who are we?"

"Well, that may take a little time to explain."

"That's all right." Judith flopped down next to him. She then snuggled up to him, while Sag rested on the floor near her like a huge footrest. "I've got lots of time."

Always willing to share stories from history with her, he began to take her on a magic carpet ride into antiquity, to a time, thousands of years ago, when the Assyrians ruled Bet Nahren with their sword.

"Daddy, is Bet Nahren very far?"

"Not too far. It is just on the other side of the mighty Zagros Mountains between the Tigris and Euphrates Rivers. It's a long stretch of land that is often called Mesopotamia."

"My teacher said the Assyrians were mean. Were they, Daddy? Were they cruel like the Turks?"

"Oh yes, and then some. Sometimes even worse. It wasn't uncommon for them to brutally kill their enemies, then flay and hang their bodies on poles outside the city walls for everyone to see."

She pushed herself away from him, and her pretty face twisted into an expression of disgust. "That's just too awful to imagine. Why would *anyone* do such horrible things?"

"For propaganda," he said. "It was a warning to others of what could happen to them if they didn't submit to Assyrian domination."

She covered her ears with her palms. "Don't tell me any more," she said. "I don't want to hear another word. All this time I thought we were *good* people. And now you tell me this."

"See the painting on the wall?" he said to her. "In 33 AD, those three apostles wiped away our ancient past by bringing the Word of God to the people. After that, nothing has ever been the same for us again."

She gazed at the painting, as though for the first time. "So that's what the picture is about?"

"That's right, Judith. Those three men are the three saints responsible for the founding of the first Christian church. The scene in that painting marks the beginning of a great new Assyrian Empire – not a military one as before, but a Christian one based on the Word of God."

She smiled with relief. "Then we aren't bad people after all."

"That's right, Judith. We proved that by creating a brilliant culture, based on the Word of God, that lasted for hundreds of years – until that fanatical Muslim, Tamerlane the Mongol, crushed it in the fourteenth century."

"What an evil thing to do!"

"You're right. It was. Tamerlane was a ruthless savage, obsessed with destroying Christianity. To survive, many Assyrians had to marry and convert to Mohammedanism. The fortunate ones escaped to other lands. As a result of mixed marriages and cultural assimilation, many Assyrians eventually lost all connection to their past."

"Does that mean us too, Daddy?" she said, startled.

"It's possible. In fact, for all we know, we could be related to some savage mountain tribe which was converted to Christianity hundreds of years ago. The only thing I can tell you with certainty about the Shamash family is that both your grandfathers and great-grandfathers were all born-again Christians who lived in the Plain for a long, long time."

"You mean," she said, horrified, "our ancestors could've been Kurds or Turks?"

"That's right."

She jumped to her feet. Sag rose up beside her. "Oh, Daddy, that's just too horrible to consider."

"Then don't think about it," he said. "And by all means don't ever bring up the subject with your granddaddy. He'll drive you crazy with his lectures on our ancestral past. Promise?"

"Yes, Daddy, I promise."

"So it's our little secret," her father said.

She looked at him, smiling affectionately. "Yes, Daddy. It's our little secret." She paused, and unexpectedly her pretty face wrinkled into a frown. "You don't think those Muslims will bother us again, do you?"

"Don't you worry about them," he said. "If they do, I'll be here to protect you."

"You don't need to protect me, Daddy," she said confidently. "I've got Sag. You take care of Mamma." She then gave her father a kiss on the lips and hurried towards the door. Sag followed, wagging his tail.

Before she could reach the door, Saliba, her father's manservant, stepped into the room and announced to Malko that Sardar Jamshid was here to see him.

A tall and handsome man entered the room. He was dressed elegantly in European style, wearing a bow tie, vest and jacket. When Judith gazed up at the man, Malko saw immediately that she was charmed by the sight of the blue-eyed and dark-haired governor. "You must be Judith," the Governor said to her, flashing a generous smile.

"That's right." She made a little curtsy. "I am Judith Shamash." she turned to her dog. "And this is my companion, Sag." She then said, "Say hello to the Sardar, Sag. Go on, Sag, shake the nice governor's hand."

Sag didn't lift his paw as he was trained to do. Instead, he just sat on his hind legs in front of Judith, separating her and the Governor, and stared at the latter menacingly. Judith appeared perplexed by Sag's uncharacteristic behavior. "Sag, be polite," she said, crouching beside Sag. "Shake hands with the man." She lifted the dog's paw, but Sag stubbornly resisted. The Governor bent forwards to pet the dog, but immediately pulled back when the dog showed its teeth and growled.

"What's wrong with you, Sag?" she scolded the dog. "That isn't how you greet a visitor."

Her father hurried to his daughter's side. "Why don't you and Sag go and play?" he said, guiding her into the hall. "The Governor has some important matters to discuss with me."

"Charming young lady," he said to Malko, watching her and the dog leave. "She is going to make some lucky man very happy."

"Hopefully he'll be a good Christian boy," Malko said, then added to make a point, "one of similar age."

The Governor nodded most graciously. "But of course."

Malko closed the door after the Governor entered the room, and he immediately changed the subject to the purpose of the visit.

Chapter 5

The Village of Thieves, the Zagros Mountains

How could such a beautiful young girl be hidden from the Governor for so long? All these years, she was right under his nose – and she slipped past him unnoticed. Then, at the most unexpected moment, when his jaded heart believed no one like her could ever exist, she suddenly appeared, a vision of beauty and innocence.

From the moment he first saw her, the Governor knew she was the one. Although they had only a brief encounter in her father's library, she still managed to leave a memorable impression.

When she smiled at him with such charm and confidence, he immediately realized that she wasn't an ordinary young lady. She was a ripe and delicious woman ready to be enjoyed. It took only those few moments of contact to convince him that he had to possess her and make her his Scheherazade, the woman who would fill his life with one thousand and one magical nights of pleasure.

In his haste to see her again, he sent the family an invitation for a party. But to his surprise and annoyance, her parents quickly sent their polite regrets.

Although there were religious differences, which occasionally led to misunderstandings between him and the Christians, it was rare for an Assyrian family to permit that to get in the way of social contact. Most wealthy Christian families were wise enough to know that there might come a time when they would need him, and it would be imprudent to do anything to offend him.

So he knew the family's decision wasn't because of religious differences, but because he had revealed too much interest in Judith. That would explain why Malko made a point of saying that he sought a good Christian boy for her, *about her age*. In his polite but direct way, Malko was telling the Governor that she was not available to him.

Well, if that Christian swine thinks he can discourage me that easily, he is gravely mistaken. There are other ways to get what I want – with or without the Shamash family's approval.

While riding with his two henchmen to the Village of the Thieves in the Zagros Mountains, he began plotting.

It was early evening when they reached the village. Seeing the village houses light up one by one, the Governor knew the Kurds were awakening from a long day's sleep, after a night of pillaging villages near the edge of the mountains. The Governor immediately prepared himself for the meeting by shifting his focus from Judith to the purpose of his journey.

Ejder met the Governor at the entrance to his home. His long cape caught the wind and flew behind him. With his leather-like skin and visibly sharp teeth, it gave him the appearance of a winged animal in flight. Instead of frightening the Governor with shrieking sounds and sharp talons, Ejder stunned him with his nauseating breath. To add to the Governor's immediate discomfort, Ejder was a big, strong man. When he hugged the Governor, Ejder hugged him tightly, to the point of pain.

"It's been a long time, Sardar, since we've seen each other, " he said after releasing the Governor from his hold. "Are those Christians giving you problems again?"

"No, not this time. This time, my friend, I'm here to tell you about my visit to Constantinople."

"That must have been a very important visit for you to want to travel so far to tell me about it," Ejder said. "Come inside where we can talk more comfortably."

It was a large, one-room house, filled with expensive spoils from his raids. On the wall or leaning against it were old ivory Persian miniatures, including several outstanding paintings and archeological relics. His mud floor was covered with two large Persian rugs with complicated floral designs in varying but pleasing colors. The rugs had been softened over the years by wear. The Governor sat down on a pillow, surrounded by the floral motif of the thick-pile rug. Smelling the lamb stew that was being prepared on the stove nearby, he began to feel hungry.

"I see you have some new acquisitions," the Governor said, admiring Ejder's home.

"I met a Christian farmer who was hoarding antiques," Ejder said with amusement. "And I persuaded him to share some with me."

The Governor laughed; he knew how persuasive Ejder could be when he demonstrated his saber skills. "I should join you on your travels. They seem to be more lucrative than collecting *baksheesh*."

After some polite conversation, Ejder signaled his wife to bring them some tea. She served the sweetened black tea with a plate of meze, which was followed by a lamb and vegetable stew; the meal ended with an assortment of cookies and honeysweet pastries. After serving the two men, she disappeared into a corner of the room and ate silently while the men smoked their hookahs.

Smoke streamed from Ejder's nose and mouth, giving him the illusion of being some wild beast on fire. "Now tell me, my friend," Ejder said. "What do I owe this pleasure to?"

"I had a long visit with Demir Pasha."

"What did the great man have to say?"

"He wants your assistance."

"My assistance? Has my fame traveled *that* far?"

"I made certain. I took it with me to the Porte."

"You are a very kind friend," Ejder said. "But why? What use could I possibly be to the Pasha?"

"He needs men like you, men from the mountain villages, to help him drive the Christians away from the Plain."

"Are you serious?" Ejder said. "How could he ever expect me to achieve such a feat? I have no army to fight the Russians." The Governor then told Ejder the Pasha's plans for removing the Russians from the Plain.

"When the last Russian leaves the Plain to head north," he said in conclusion, "that will be your signal to attack and to cleanse the area of infidels. You will have the Pasha's German-trained army units as your backup."

Ejder listened thoughtfully, then said: "Tell me, Sardar, what's in it for me? How much?"

"Anything and everything you can grab."

Ejder expression filled with greed. "That could be a very nice haul," he smiled. "Those Christians love to hoard gold."

"Then you're interested?"

"Let me talk to some of my friends. They may like the idea and may want to join me." He turned to the Eunuch guarding the door and snapped his fingers. "Now that that's settled, let's have some entertainment. How about a sweet treat – an untouched Assyrian girl? I got several last night. Maybe one will please you?"

Before the Governor could respond, the eunuch brought two frightened girls into the room and shoved them to floor for inspection.

The Eunuch yanked their heads up by the hair so the Governor could see their faces. "Pretty, aren't they? Take one. She's yours for the night."

The Governor shook his head. He was thinking about Judith. "Not tonight. Tonight I am too tired from my journey."

"Very well. But before you retire, let me prepare you for some sweet dreams."

After the Eunuch left with the Assyrian girls, Ejder clapped his hands. A bare-footed woman scantily clad in crimson burst into the room, startling the Governor. She was holding a long, red silk scarf, which was flying in the air behind her. The dancer quickly positioned herself in front of the Governor and began to shiver and shimmy her hips to the beat of the percussions of the six-piece band that followed behind her.

When she had the Governor's complete attention and his gaze was focused on her quick-moving hips, she suddenly stopped all movement, thrust her breasts before him so he could admire them, and froze. After a sufficient pause, the wind and string instruments began to play a melody, and she slowly thawed and came to life again. Her movements were sinuous and graceful; the stylized twists and turns of her arms, legs, and head were designed to draw attention to each part of her body. When she had completely mesmerized him, she made a circle in the air with her scarf and wrapped herself in it with a spin, covering her entire body with a red, translucent, silky layer of fabric. Then she gave the scarf a sudden yank and spun on her toes, before collapsing in a bow in front of the Governor.

The Governor observed her, impressed, while smoking his hookah. When she finished, he thanked her, then excused himself and retired for the evening. His dreams were not of the seductive dancer who promised him a night of endless pleasure, but instead of the sweet nymphet, Judith.

Chapter 6

The Village of Shamash

Malko was proud of the *Zahria-d-Bahra* newspaper that he and his two friends published. After months of carefully debating the practicality of starting a newspaper, Malko finally convinced the two men that the Plain was ready to hear their combined voices, and a few weeks later they published their first issue.

To make certain everyone understood their mission, he summarized it on the newspaper's masthead for everyone to see. "*Zahria-d-Bahra* will publish all articles of local and international interest, addressing both secular and non-secular issues of specific relevance to the residents in the 250 villages clustered near the Nazlu, Shahar and Baranduz Rivers. Like the three rivers that flow eastward irrigating the land from the Zagros Mountains to Lake Urmia, *Zahria-d-Bahra* will spread the light in the Plain by providing its readers with an understanding and an awareness of the contemporary world."

Once a week, Malko met with his two partners at his home to discuss the editorial content of the upcoming issue. Today's weekly meeting centered on the recent abduction of two girls and the looting and burning of a village at the foot of the Zagros Mountains.

Malko's father-in-law, the Reverend Daniel Tamras, was the first to voice his opinion. He was particularly upset about this recent raid led by the Kurds. The moment the subject came up he exploded with righteous indignation. "It's outrageous!" Daniel said. "This time those vermin have gone too far." His pince-nez, which sat precariously on his nose, fell into his hand. He quickly put the glasses back on his nose. "This mustn't continue. We mustn't allow that mountain trash to abduct and dishonor our women at will. We must stop them, *immediately.*"

"I agree with you, father," Malko said to Daniel. "But we've got to remember this is a delicate issue. If we tell our readers what we think they ought to do, we will anger the Mohammedans. If we ignore our responsibility, we will only give those savages a license to repeat their crime."

Joel Yohanna, a wealthy landowner from Gulpashan and a graduate of Yale University, was a man who always weighed both sides of an argument in order to reach a reasonable solution. For the first time, he had no suggestions. "So what do we do?" Joel asked. "We can't negotiate with them – it would only give respectability to their actions, and we can't sit back and ignore them. As you said, Malko, it would only give them a license to repeat their crimes. That leaves us at an impasse."

Malko knew if one of those girls were Judith, nothing would stop him from pursuing those kidnappers. Why should it be any different in this case?

"You're wrong, Joel," Malko said. "There is something we can do."

"What's that?" Joel asked.

"Take covert and decisive action."

Joel glanced at Malko curiously. "Would you like to explain yourself?"

"It's very simple," Malko said. "I will form a posse and go after them."

"That's madness!" his father-in-law erupted. Once again his glasses fell from his nose. This time he placed them in the lapel pocket of his clerical black jacket without interrupting his thought. "You can't take such a chance, son. Those jackals will kill you."

"I can, and I will."

"What are you going to fight them with?" Daniel snapped sarcastically. "Twigs and knives?"

"With guns, of course."

"Guns?" Daniel said, shocked. "You have guns? Where did you get them?"

"I've been buying them secretly from the Russians for months and quietly arming the villagers."

"You told the Governor you had no guns," Daniel said, "that to the best of your knowledge no one in the village had guns."

"I said that for obvious reasons. If I hadn't, he would have thought of some way to confiscate them – and we would be helpless at defending ourselves in an emergency."

"But he'll find out. Surely he will. He has spies everywhere."

"Eventually, I suspect. But by that time there will be an open war, and it will be too late for him to do anything."

"Regardless, I won't permit it. It's too dangerous and overt," Daniel said to him. He was behaving like a father addressing a disobedient son. His voice was loud and mighty for such a small man, and it resonated clearly throughout the room. "The Governor will find out the minute you attack that village, and he will know you lied to him. God only knows what he'll do then."

"He won't find out," Malko said. "We will attack at night. No one will recognize us."

"Daniel's right, Malko," Joel said. "The Governor will find out. He has spies everywhere. Everything we do is discovered by him – and the Royal Family in Teheran."

"That's the chance we must take, Joel. Now, here's my plan," Malko said. "We will start a new column. We can call it 'Our Daily Prayer,' and we can use it to feature subjects to pray about. It will be our code page for alerting the Assyrians to what is happening in the Plain and what we must do."

"Very clever," Joel smiled.

"We can introduce this column with an article about those abducted girls." Malko added. "My men and I will do the rest ourselves tonight."

That day Malko and his armed posse set off in the darkness to raid the Village of Thieves. Lodged on the Persian side of the Zagros Mountains, the village had a notorious reputation for hiding criminals. It lay in a small area of the mountains where the river passed on its journey to Lake Urmia. Most Urmians reportedly avoided this area out of fear for their lives. Gruesome stories of what the Kurds did to anyone discovered near the village were always circulating in the Plain as a warning to Urmians to maintain their distance.

When Malko and his posse arrived at the village, it was evening, and the stone and clay houses were beginning to light up. The Kurds who slept by day were rising to prepare for a "day of work." Convinced their reputation protected them from unwanted visitors, they were unprepared to defend themselves against Malko and his men, who descended upon them unexpectedly on horseback with rifles slung over their backs, brandishing their swords. In the moonlight, the posse was a terrifying sight, as dangerous-looking as the ancient Assyrian warriors might have been. Frightened, the Kurds reacted just as Malko had expected. They scattered into the night. Without a gunshot, Malko and his men were able to rescue the young girls and reclaim the stolen property.

In the column entitled "Our Daily Prayer," Malko prepared a sub-heading, "The Miracle of Prayer." It contained a thank you to God for answering their prayers and returning the abducted girls safely to their village.

Malko knew his modest military success was insufficient to stop the Kurds. As a long-time servant of history, he had learned that their hatred against Christians was too deep to be checked with just one quick strike. These people were driven by savage instincts, not reason. It would require a mighty act to bring them to their knees.

"This is only the beginning," he told his father-in-law during a private conversation. "As long as the Persian government imprisons us like criminals on this small stretch of land, we will always be an easy target for our enemies."

"I know, my son. Still, I am very proud of you," Daniel said. "You risked your life to save those two girls, and despite the odds, you succeeded."

"I had to act, Father. I shudder when I think what would've happened to them if I hadn't helped them," his voice grew solemn. *"One of them could've easily been Judith."*

"You did the right thing, Malko. I feel foolish for having objected to your plan."

"Unfortunately, my actions don't change anything, Father," Malko said. "Our circumstances still remain the same. Our enemy still lurks nearby."

"That's true. But remember, there is a limit to what they can do. This is Persia, not Turkey. The

Shah is too sensitive to international opinion to allow anything serious to happen to us."

"You are correct, Father," Malko replied. "As long as we are useful to the Royal Family, we will be safe. The moment we cease to provide a political and trade advantage for Teheran in its negotiations with the Christian nations, anything is possible. Have no doubts about it. The Mohammedans have no real love for us."

"It really doesn't matter. We still have the Russians."

"But for how long?" Malko said. "Right now, Tsar Nicholas is dealing with severe social unrest within his own country, which he can barely control. What would happen to us if it got out of hand and his empire collapsed? Who would protect us then?"

"If it ever came to that," Daniel said, "then we would have only two choices – to leave it in God's hands or to run."

Malko gazed out the window, past the orchard bordering the Shahar River, at the land that had belonged to his ancestors, an ancient land rich in history, layered with memories that stretched back thousands of years before Christ. In this fertile region that was his home, he was surrounded by the beauty of the Syriac language, the same language Jesus had spoken; and he walked on land, the same land that Jesus might have walked on. Where else but here could he be so close to his Christian roots?

"You are right. We must leave it in His hands," Malko said. "When the time comes to act, God will show us the way."

He thought about the Kurds perched on the mountain edge, eying the prosperity of the Christians with envy. He knew, if given the opportunity, they would spring from their hideaways like a pack of jackals and devour everything in sight. He wondered if this was the right time for him and his family to leave the Plain.

Like many women born to comfort, Abigail needed suitable work to lend purpose to her life. Unlike her sister-in-law, Suzy, who was a nurse, she had no professional training. To avoid feeling useless, she would give Bible lessons based on what her father had taught her.

Several times a week, Abigail would join Suzy and visit nearby Mohammedan villages, where she would read and tell stories from the Bible to the local women. To many of these women, sold into marriage at an early age, Abigail offered a glimpse into a bright new world, a world in which they were equal in God's eyes to men rather than soulless creatures, as they were taught, born only to serve. During these afternoons when she was reading the Scriptures to the women, she felt her life had purpose, and this was how the Lord wanted her to serve Him.

Many of the women appreciated her uplifting stories from the Bible. After exhausting themselves carrying sacks of grain or fruit on their back all morning, the women enjoyed the opportunity to rest under a shaded fruit tree next to Abigail while she told them stories from the Bible. As they listened peacefully to Abigail, while breast-feeding their babies, soothed by the warm afternoon breeze, Suzy would attend to their medical needs.

During one such visit, a woman unexpectedly collapsed in the field. Her companion lifted her and led her to a shaded tree. Suzy, a diminutive woman with a gentle but no-nonsense demeanor, immediately went up to her.

"You should be at home, resting," Suzy scolded the woman after examining her. "You continue to work like this, and you'll have a miscarriage." A bruise peeked out from beneath her head scarf. Suzy removed the scarf and saw a cut and a large bluish black mark. "How did that happen?"

The woman looked away, ashamed. "I hit my head."

"You mean your husband hit you?"

"No, no," she said, embarrassed. "I lost my balance and hit my head."

"Let me take you home. You must rest." "But I have to work," she protested.

"Of course you do," Suzy said. "But you must also take care of yourself." Suzy felt her forehead. "You're running a fever. Let me take you to the American Hospital and have you examined."

The woman panicked. "No," she protested. "I'll be all right!"

"But you need medical attention."

"I don't want to go to the hospital. Please don't take me there. I beg you. *Please.*"

Working alongside Suzy, Abigail learned quickly that many Mohammedans believed the hospital was a place to die, not a place to heal. Despite the American Mission Hospital's fine reputation in the Plain, it was almost impossible to convince them otherwise.

"We can take you to my doctor," Abigail suggested. "He will be happy to examine you."

"I have no money," the woman said with shame. "My husband takes it all."

"Don't worry," Abigail said. "Dr Benyamin is my friend. He won't charge you."

Later, when Suzy and Abigail were alone, relaxing and drinking tea in the parlor, Abigail said to Suzy ruefully: "Those women really suffer. I don't know how they endure."

"It isn't just the Mohammedans, Abigail. Many Christian women face their own hell as well. Did you and my brother ever see the play, *The Deserter*?"

"Yes, we did. Several days ago, in fact," Abigail said. "Malko and I took your advice and saw it."

"What did you think?"

"I was impressed. The playwright certainly understands the plight of Christian women."

"Yes, I agree," Suzy said. "Unfortunately, he doesn't go anywhere with it. The story needs a strong resolution."

Abigail set her tea glass down and crossed her legs at the ankles. "You know," she said, leaning toward Suzy, "that's exactly what I said to the playwright."

"Bravo, my dear sister," Suzy said. "And what did he say?"

"He agreed."

"Is that all? He just agreed?"

"Well, he did say he thought about doing a sequel, but he hesitated. He thinks it might be a little too risky," Abigail said. "A play about a man deserting his wife is one thing. A play with a positive resolution is an entirely different matter. I tried to reason with him. I even told him that if he agreed to write a sequel with a suitable ending, I would be willing to commission him."

"Did he reconsider?"

"He said he would think about it."

"That's encouraging."

"I think he was just dismissing me. I'm sure he's afraid to go any further with the subject."

"That's the problem these days, Abigail. No one will take a stand."

"So what do we do? How do we change that? Improving women's circumstances isn't going to be easy without assistance. The only way we can reduce the mass exodus of men from Persia is to provide them with an opportunity to make a decent living. But the unfair tax laws against Christians make it difficult for the *rayats* to do that."

That evening she posed the question to Malko. "There's no question about it, Abigail," Malko said to Abigail. "The Governor is seriously contributing to this exodus by taxing us severely on everything – from our land to our herd. But do you really believe writing about it in a play will change that?"

"It could," she said. "He might wake up and realize that by reducing our taxes he could slow down the mass exodus of workers. This would give the tax collectors a larger population to tax, and it would halt the grumbling of the *rayats* who feel they aren't making enough profit for all their labor."

"Your reasoning is excellent," he said. "But I fear if your idea is put into practice it will only backfire."

"But how?" she asked, confused.

"First, telling the Governor to reduce taxes will only anger him. Second, and most importantly, if he agreed and you got your way, it would only encourage Christians to remain here in the Plain, where their future is uncertain. Such a decision could set them up for a tragedy far greater than any they could possibly face struggling in a new country."

She went silent. How could she argue with him? Malko always knew how to cut to the point. His interest in the subject didn't end when she fell silent; he continued thinking about it as they were preparing for bed. She got the first clue when he mentioned a letter he had received from his brother in California.

"Dakan said the San Joaquin Valley is quite beautiful at this time of year, not too different, in fact, from what we know in the Plain."

"I am sure it is." She freed her long black hair, which had been rolled up above her neck into a neat bun, and let it fall to her waist. She then began to brush it. By paying more attention to her hair than the conversation, Abigail hoped she would be able to avoid an open discussion of the subject.

He tried again, pushing his point persistently. "Dakan says he is growing everything he needs – walnuts, grapes, oranges, and…"

She placed the brush down on the dressing table and turned towards him. "I know where you're heading with this, Malko," she said with a hint of impatience. "I still haven't changed my mind. Dakan is a coward. He ran to America for safety, and I re-fuse to be like him and do the same."

"He isn't a coward, Abigail. It took courage for him to leave Persia and go to America and start a new life."

"Perhaps, but it takes even more courage to do what we are doing – staying here and resisting."

"Today," he said ruefully, "that may no longer be a sensible option. Our world is falling apart. Those two girls who were abducted should be our reminder of what could easily happen to our child at anytime."

Fear came over her, the fear of a mother for the safety of her daughter. "That's a frightening thought, Malko Shamash," she said. "I don't want to hear another word about it."

"You must face the facts, Abigail. We have an enemy at our border, waiting to crush us. To make matters worse, we have a corrupt governor who is always looking for new ways to enrich himself. Anything is possible, anytime."

"But I thought you were taking care of him? That he wasn't a problem anymore?"

"Yes, I am, with a little *baksheesh* from time to time," he said. "But I fear that isn't enough. I sense he wants *more*. When he visited me recently, he strongly recommended that we and the others turn in our guns."

"How does he know you've got guns? You never told him, did you?"

"Of course not. I would never be that foolish. Without guns to protect us, we would be at his mercy, and we can't give him that advantage. I am sure he suspects we have an arsenal, and he wants to confiscate it. Fortunately, there isn't much he can do at this time, because of the Russians. But that could always change. Maybe that's what he expects. Believe me, he is planning something, something treacherous. I can feel it when I am in his presence."

"So what are you suggesting? We pack and run?"

"That is a possible solution."

"But not a very practical one, Malko. We will lose everything we have." She rose and went up to him. He was ready to say something. She put her finger on his lips. "No more talk on the subject. We both love the Plain too much to leave now. Later, if it becomes necessary, we can discuss it again at length. For now, our little *méchante* and I want to remain here by your side in Shamash."

To discourage further conversation, even though she knew they needed to talk, she put her arms around Malko and distracted him with her embrace.

Abigail never told Malko. In fact, she never told anyone, especially her parents, about her love for Dakan. What stopped her from eloping with him, when he proposed fourteen years ago, wasn't family tradition or the unpardonable sin of *jelawtha*, or her love for Persia. It was more complicated than that.

"I can't leave, Dakan," she had said when they were alone together in the cloakroom of the Shamash Presbyterian Church. "The Plain is my home."

He held her close and tight, hidden from view in a small room filled with winter coats. "Forget the Plain," he said. "We will build a new home together in America."

"It won't be the same."

"Of course, it won't," he said impatiently, his strong male personality agitated by her refusal to yield to his will. "Does everything have to be the same for you to appreciate it?"

"You're missing the point. I want to be here. I want to be *close* to my roots."

"There's nothing here, Abigail, just history-book memories. In America, we will have a future – opportunities unlike anything we know in Persia."

"You're wrong, Dakan. We have a name and a heritage that will provide us with everything we need."

"We are also Christians. Need I remind you what the Sultan did to the Armenians?"

"This is Persia, not Turkey. We are safe here."

"Yes, but for how long?"

"For as long as we will fight for it."

"I'm sorry, Abigail. There's nothing here worth fighting for."

"What about me? Am I not worth fighting for?"

"Of course, you are."

"Then stay with me, Dakan. Let's begin our life together here."

"Have you forgotten? You're promised to Malko. Our parents would never allow it."

"We can talk to them. They'll understand."

"Do you really expect me to stay here, where I will be Malko's younger brother, always living in his financial shadow?"

"Forget his money. We can build on what you already have. Together we've got all we need – two great family names, the Tamrases and the Shamashes, and enough money to build a prosperous future. We don't need more."

"I'm sorry, Abigail. It won't work for me. If that's what you want, you should stay here and marry Malko. You will get the family name – and his money as well."

"But I want you!"

"I am afraid you can't have me on your terms, Abigail. I am going to America, and that's final."

"I hate you, Dakan Shamash," she said angrily. "You're *impossibly* unreasonable. Go to America. See if I care." She turned her head away from him and buried her face in a fur coat to smother her sob.

"Stop trying to manipulate me, Abigail. It won't work."

He yanked her close and held her firmly, a man claiming what he felt was rightfully his. He then kissed her. The forbidden excitement of the embrace mingled recklessly with her anger created an explosive moment of passion she found impossible to control.

"Come with me, Abigail," he whispered tenderly. "We will have a wonderful life together in America."

She was being swept away again by her emotion, guided by his will, when she heard her mother and father talking in the vestibule. The sound of their voices interrupted her moment of abandonment, and she awoke abruptly to reality.

"I wonder where Abigail went," her mother was saying. "She was talking to Dakan just a few minutes ago and then they both disappeared."

"You worry too much, Miriam," Abigail's father said. "She's probably with the others in the recreation room."

Abigail pulled away from Dakan. The magic of the moment was gone. Guilt had broken through, filling her with panic. "They mustn't find us together like this," she said. "It'll disgrace them."

"Forget them, Abigail. It's you and me. That's all that matters." He kissed her again, and she began to dissolve in his arms. Frightened that she might lose control, she pushed him away and ran from the cloakroom into the arms of her mother who was returning to the vestibule.

"There you are," her mother said," I've been looking for you everywhere."

Abigail was crying when she collapsed into her mother's arms. "There, there, child," Miriam said. "It can't be that bad."

Dakan walked past them and paused for a moment before leaving the church. He stared at Abigail beseechingly. During that split second, while their gazes locked, Dakan and Abigail's iron wills resumed their battle. Once again neither of them was strong enough to defeat the other.

"Take me home, Mother." Abigail said. "I want to go home."

Dakan left for America the following day without writing or visiting her. He just disappeared. She learned about his departure from his mother over tea a few days later.

The following month she married Malko, as the family had planned.

Chapter 7

The Shamash Home

Sag ran around the orchard sniffing and digging. There were piles of dirt everywhere, miniature mountains next to shallow cavities, marking the location of where he had uncovered bones. Judith sat under a shaded tree, surrounded by the bones Sag had retrieved, and examined each one thoughtfully, as if they were important pieces of a jigsaw, which, when connected, would lead to a significant anthropological find.

Most of the bones looked alike, not very different from those the cook might have given Sag. Each one varied only slightly in size and shape, and each appeared to have been chewed. As she looked at the pile of bones, discouraged by what she had, Sag returned with another bone and dropped it on her lap. Delighted with his gift, she grabbed it and examined it closely, then sprang to her feet. This one was unlike all the other bones. It looked like the jaw of some primitive man – one of those savage Kurds who lived in mountain caves that her granddaddy always spoke about.

She excitedly waved the bone in front of Sag's face. "Where did you find it, Sag?" she asked him. "Show me, Sag. Show me."

Exhausted, Sag collapsed to the ground near Judith, his long tongue hanging from one side of his mouth, and looked up at her, totally indifferent to her command. She patted her hip. "Come, Sag. Show me." The dog dropped his head, resting it on one leg, too tired to play this game anymore. "Please Sag," she said. The urgency of her tone caught his attention, and he reluctantly rose and led her to a hole beneath an apple tree, where he dropped to the ground to rest in the shade. Judith examined the hole but found nothing. She began to dig into the hole with her hands, and she still found nothing.

Discouraged, she gazed around the orchard. *Where could he have found it? Which one of those holes hid the other skeletal remains?* She knew that if she did find the spot, she might uncover the rest of the head – and maybe even some important clues to the Shamash past. *What a find that would be. I can see it now. Anthropologist Judith Shamash discovers primitive man – the link connecting all Assyrians to their ancestral origin. Oh, how exciting that would be!*

She hurried about the orchard inspecting all the holes Sag had made and frantically dug deeper into them, clawing at the earth with her fingers. Exhausted from her efforts, she returned to her pile of bones and sat under the tree. She looked at the mess she had made in the orchard. *Daddy will be furious when he sees what I've done,* she thought. *But he'll understand. I'm sure he'll understand, once I show him what Sag and I uncovered.*

But where are the other remains? There's got to be more. Her gaze canvassed the orchard again, as though she were sure it would halt at just the exact spot where the jawbone had been found. *What would an anthropologist do in my situation?* She asked herself. *Dig deeper, of course. Get a shovel and dig until he found the skull that goes with the jaw. But where do I begin?*

It would take days, maybe even weeks, of digging, before I could find anything else, not to mention all the holes I would have to make. If only I were sure Sag had taken me to the right spot, then I could fill the other holes and just dig in that spot.

As she sat under the tree, pondering her problem, she heard a disapproving voice address her. "Young lady," the voice said, "What, in heaven's name, are you doing?"

She jerked her head towards the voice. It was grandfather. He was dressed in black as usual, and he was carrying a Bible and a note pad. Aware of his routine, she suspected he had just returned from the river shore, where he went for his daily meditation.

"I'm searching for bones."

"I see that. But why?"

"I'm looking for a skull."

"A skull? What makes you think there's a skull in your father's orchard?"

"This." She presented him with the jawbone Sag had uncovered. "What do you think, Granddaddy?

Do you think it's a missing link, that it belongs to one of our ancient relatives – one of those Kurds or Turks?"

"A Kurd or Turk, our relative!? *Outrageous!*" he said, his pince-nez falling from his nose. "Where did you ever get such an idea?" He caught the glasses in motion and placed them back on his nose.

"Daddy said…" She stopped and covered her mouth with her hand. "Ooops!"

"Well, finish your sentence, Judith. What did your daddy say?"

She hesitated and gazed at the stack of bones beside her.

"Judith, will you kindly answer me? What did your daddy say?"

"Well, Daddy said…" She stopped, unable to continue. She couldn't break her promise to her father; yet at the same time she couldn't disrespect her grandfather by refusing to answer his question.

"Judith," he said insistently. "I'm still waiting."

She was trapped and totally incapable of fighting her grandfather's will. Knowing him, he would not relent until he got a full explanation. There was nothing she could do but surrender. "Well, he said that all of us are related and we belong to one single family. I thought if I could find an original link I could prove his idea."

"*Just as I thought.* He's been reading Darwin again. For the record, *and don't you ever forget this*, Judith Shamash, we have no blood connection whatsoever with those savages. We are Christians, and have been since the dawn of Christianity. Is that clear?"

"Yes, Granddaddy," she said obediently. She then added with an urgent plea, "Promise me you won't tell Daddy that I told you. He will be angry with me. Please, Granddaddy, *promise*."

Daniel yielded to her plea and smiled gently. "Very well, Judith, but you've got to promise me something in return."

"What's that, Granddaddy?"

"I don't want to hear any more nonsense like that from you again."

"Yes, Granddaddy," she said obediently. Before he could make her promise anything else, she swiftly changed the subject. "Well, what do you think of the bone? Do you think it's very old?"

He silently examined it, turning it from side to side, and nodded when he was finished. "Oh yes, very old."

"As old as Adam and Eve?"

"I doubt that it's that old. True, we do live in the Fertile Crescent, and true, it is possible that Adam and Eve may have wandered here at some point. But to imagine it to be that old would be stretching things a bit."

"But it is old, Granddaddy. You are sure of that."

"It looks old to me. But we better leave that to the experts to decide," he said. "Would you like me to show it to my friend at the university to get his opinion?"

She jumped to her feet, excited. "Would you, Granddaddy? That would be wonderful. When you do, please don't forget to tell him who I am. I want everyone to know what I discovered."

"If this turns out to be an important find, you may become a very famous young lady – with your story in history books for everyone to read. Would you like that?"

She was ready to explode with joy. "Oh yes, very much."

His tone changed as he gazed around the orchard. "Before you get all excited about becoming famous, I think you better start filling up all those holes – before your father discovers them and gives you a good spanking."

"But if I do that," she said, "how will I ever know where to look again, if this jaw turns out to be an important find?"

"Excellent point," he said, impressed. "Here's my solution. Fill all the holes, and mark each spot with a stick and a red ribbon."

"Thanks, Granddaddy. That's a wonderful idea."

Judith was playing with her dolls in her room when her mother entered and sat down on a chair near her. It was obvious from her mother's expression that something was deeply bothering her. Judith wondered if it had anything to do with a promise Judith forgot to keep. Since she made so many each week, it was impossible to remember them all.

"Is something wrong, Mamma?" Judith asked nervously.

Her mother handed her the newspaper she was holding.

"Have you seen this week's *University Bulletin*?"

"No, Mamma."

"Well, for a start, there's an article in it about you."

"Me, Mamma?" She eagerly grabbed the *Bulletin* her mother handed her. "Is it about the bone I found?"

"It is," she said gravely.

Her tone cooled Judith's excitement. She nervously read the article, fearful it might contain information that would embarrass or harm the family. Her mother observed Judith as she read.

Thirteen-year-old Judith Shamash, daughter of prominent landowner Malko Shamash, this week made an extraordinary anthropological discovery in her father's orchard. She unearthed a jawbone that local scientists believe to have belonged to Paleolithic man. If this proves correct, it will be one of the earliest traces of human life ever uncovered in the Plain.

According to Judith's report, she and her dog were digging in her father's orchard for ancient artifacts when her dog surprised her by delivering what appeared to be a human jawbone. If scientific evidence confirms what local experts believe is true, this jawbone could date back to the Pleistocene period. It might even be the same age as the Heidelberg skull found in Germany in 1907. The two finds share striking similarities – small teeth and a large jaw.

Local experts are unable to pinpoint the exact age of the find, but they believe that it could possibly be a million or more years old. Paleolithic man was a river hunter, and the property where it was found is located on the edge of the Shahar River.

The jawbone will be on exhibit in the historical museum at Urmia University.

After reading the article, Judith was confused by her mother's concern. There was nothing in it that could be considered damaging or embarrassing. It was straightforward and factual. "What's wrong, Mamma? Don't you like the article?"

"It isn't the article, Judith," her mother said with concern. "It's the photograph. Didn't I tell you, you mustn't pose for photographs?"

"But the newspaper man didn't take the photograph. That's the one you took of me at Lake Urmia," she said. "Remember, you thought it was funny how ghostly white I looked after swimming in the silvery salt water. See," she said, pointing to the pictures. "That's the one he published."

"Did you ever ask yourself why I didn't want your picture published?"

Judith shook her head.

"Because I don't want strangers to recognize you."

Judith remained confused. "No one will recognize me, Mamma. That picture doesn't even look like me."

"It looks enough like you to be of concern."

Judith couldn't grasp why her mother was so concerned about a photograph. She never thought that giving the reporter an amusing picture of her at the lake would ever become a problem. Nothing in her mother's expression provided Judith with any clue as to why she objected to it. "Aren't you proud of what Sag and I uncovered?"

"Mon ange," her mother said gently, "it has nothing to do with what you and Sag discovered. Yes, I think it is wonderful that you have found such an old jawbone. Yes, I am proud that it will be on display at the museum with your name on it. But what concerns me – and I can't stress this enough – is that these are difficult times, and I don't want others to recognize you as the daughter – and a very beautiful daughter – of a wealthy Assyrian landowner. It will give the wrong people the wrong ideas."

"You mean," Judith said, disappointed, "I will never be able to have my picture in the newspaper again?"

"For now, no," her mother said. "Maybe when you're older, and times are better, then it will be acceptable. For now, it must be avoided. It will only attract attention to you." She then added firmly but kindly, "Is that clear, Judith?"

"Yes, Mamma."

"I know what a willful child you are," she said. "One day this same willfulness may serve you well if wisely directed. But if you aren't careful, it can also lead to regrets. That's why I must insist you always *think* before you act. I don't want you to make any mistakes that you will later regret."

"But Mamma, I meant no harm."

"I understand that, Judith. On the surface, your decision was perfectly acceptable. But in the future, no more pictures for publication. Is that clear?"

"Yes, Mamma."

Chapter 8

The Shamash Presbyterian Church

The worshipper self-consciously slipped into the Shamash Presbyterian Church while the soloist was singing a hymn. As he tiptoed towards a back-row seat, the floorboards responded to each step with spontaneous outcries of protest. When he hit a particularly cranky board, he froze, embarrassed, and waited a few moments until he felt it was safe to continue. At that exact moment, when he was certain he could cause no further disturbance, he slowly lowered himself into an empty pew and sat rigidly still.

Unlike the others in the congregation, he wasn't dressed suitably for church, and, by comparison, he looked like someone who had spent the morning in the fields. Embarrassed at wearing such unsuitable attire, he avoided making any movement that might draw attention to him. But no matter how hard he tried, he couldn't escape the gaze of the soloist who observed him as she sang.

My heart is aching, I see the storm;
All around me, the ocean roars.

Give me strength, my Lord, to make it home;
For all around me, I see the storm.

I should've waited to enter until after she finished sing-ing, he thought. *Maybe that's what they do in Christian churches.*

A man wearing a clerical black suit stepped up to the pulpit when the soloist finished and placed a pince-nez on his nose to read from the newspaper he held. It was a passage from *Zahria-d-Bahra*, thanking readers for their prayers for the two abduct-ed girls. "Once again God listened and answered our prayers."

He cleared his throat, removed his pince-nez and began his sermon. His voice was clear and powerful, and it resonated throughout the chapel.

"Today, my friends, my sermon will be about the sins of Sultan Abdul Hamid. For nearly 30 years, this former emperor of the Ottomans, this once beloved caliph of the Faithful, this notorious *Crim-son* Sultan, bloodied his hands, inflicting on Christians untold hardship. He taxed them to extremes, shackled them with unjust laws, and punished them severely for the slightest infractions. And when they couldn't take it any longer and protested and even dared to resist, he slaughtered them without mercy, using the most savage methods imaginable and hiring the most sadistic criminals that he could find. The crimes he committed against man during his reign were so grave that even the international community had to react by threatening him with sanctions. But when the time came to apply the sanctions, what did the West do?" The Minister's gaze glided across the congregation before finally connecting with the new worshipper. "It did nothing," he said. "That's right. *Nothing*."

The stranger shook his head sadly, remembering.

"*How could this be?*" the Minister continued, as he resumed looking out across the congregation. "Thousands of innocent Christians slaughtered – *yet no one acted*. What were those world leaders thinking?" He leaned forward, his two hands resting on either side of the pulpit. "Well, my beloved friends, I'll tell you what they were thinking. *They were thinking if they brought sanctions against the Sultan, they could jeopardize their lucrative trade agreements with the Ottomans.*"

The stranger closed his eyes and took a deep breath. He remembered thinking similar thoughts.

"Tens of thousands of innocent men and women and children slaughtered by that crazed ruler, and the leaders of the West did nothing, because they wanted to protect their trade agreements with the Turks. Tell me, my friends, honestly, is there really any difference between those who commit the crime and those who ignore it?"

After the sermon ended and the last worshipper left, the young man introduced himself to the Reverend. Daniel Tamras invited him into his office, where they were able to talk privately.

"I don't recognize you, Mohamad," Daniel said. "Are you new to this area?"

"Yes, I come from a small village near Mosul."

"Are you a Christian?"

"No, Muslim."

"But I thought only the Christians were leaving Turkey?"

"That's true. The smart ones, those able to leave while they still had a chance."

"Why did you leave? You were a Muslim. Weren't you safe?"

"Yes, it's true. I was physically safe," he said. "But my conscience wasn't." He then told Daniel his story.

During most of his life, he was a good Muslim. Like all good Muslims, he faithfully followed the Five Pillars of Islam. Although he believed that Allah was the only God, he regarded the Christian God not with contempt as his mullahs had taught him, but instead with indifference. Five times a day he would pray to Allah with a series of bows, prostrations, and recitations from the Koran; every week he would give a percentage of his meager income to the poor; during Ramadan, he would avoid food and drink during daylight hours; and, like other devout Muslims, he was saving money to take a pilgrimage to Mecca and earn his Mecca Certificate. But unlike some devout Muslims, especially the militant ones, he harbored no contempt for the Christians.

"It's difficult being a decent Muslim these days," Mohamad said. "Following the Five Pillars of Islam is no longer enough. Every day we are expected to do more. You said earlier that the Sultan was an evil leader because he blooded his hands killing all those Armenians, but I have discovered that Demir Pasha isn't any better. He is achieving the same end by simply convincing the Turks that 'Turkey belongs to the Turks.' On the surface, those words sound innocent enough. But in truth they are a code for turning Muslims against non-Muslims."

"Is that why you left?"

"No, I left when I saw those words put into action." He paused before proceeding. What he was about to tell the Pastor wasn't easy. He took a deep breath to collect his strength before continuing. "It all began for me unexpectedly. I was in the fields, harvesting the crop with the other field workers, when an army of Turks descended on us and forced us from the fields at gunpoint. They then lined us up, separating the Christians from the Muslims. Those Christians who refused to renounce their faith by pronouncing *shahada* and accepting Muhammad as the only true messenger of God were immediately butchered and tossed to the animals for food."

On the surface, Mohamad was a physically strong man who toiled with his body, a man who had complete control of his emotions. But when he remembered that massacre, he found himself helplessly dissolving in grief. "They were good people, those Christians. Every one of them worked hard for what they had. Their only mistake was not being Muslims. Was that reason enough to kill them?" He lowered his head, ashamed of what was happening in his country. "It was the same everywhere I went."

"Then it's all true," Daniel said, stunned. "Everything I've heard is all true."

"It's gotten very bad, especially for clerics and other Christian leaders," Mohamad said sadly. "The Turks are getting great pleasure in slowly torturing them. The others. Well, the others are being forcefully relocated to the South. Almost every day, I would see hundreds of people herded along the road. Emaciated men, women, and children, driven from their homes, many stripped of clothing, all hungry and thirsty, and in pain from their continuous beatings. Some of them barely able to walk. Deported (who knew where?) to their death…"

"Armenians?"

"Armenians, Assyrians, Jews. It didn't matter. Anyone who was *non*-Muslim," he said. "The fortunate ones collapsed from exhaustion and were bayoneted or shot and left to rot beside the road. The others? I could only guess."

"So it has finally come down to that," Daniel said sadly.

"You are a wise man, Daniel. So tell me, please. Why, *why is* this happening? Is it simply because of religious differences?"

"No, Mohamad, it isn't because of religious differences. Many Muslims don't care what our views are about Jesus or God or the spirit after death.

Those are merely theological concerns, which have no real impact on their individual lives. And it isn't because of rising nationalism either, as some leaders are claiming. Those are just political devices to set in motion a larger plan."

"A larger plan?" Mohamad asked, alert, as the conversation took an unexpected but important turn.

"Yes, my friend. One as old as life itself."

"You mean, the original sin?"

"I prefer to call it greed, or in political jargon, *imperialism*."

Mohamad leaned back in the chair. He was thinking – searching through his experiences for the facts to support Daniel's statement. "But if you are right," he said after a long pause, "why are the Turks so savagely killing the Christians? Why don't they just claim their land and send the Christians on their way?"

"To win wars and build new empires," Daniel explained, "the enemy must be completely eliminated. For the average soldier, greed or imperialism isn't reason enough to motivate them to kill. Something important must be threatened. The Young Turks in Constantinople know this. That's why they carefully cultivate religious hatred. Mixed with propaganda, religion can be used as an effective 'moral' weapon against the Christians. With Allah on their side, how can anything they do be wrong?"

"You make it sound so evil and calculating."

"That's because it is."

"What will become of us? How will this all end?"

"You will find the answer to that in the Book of Revelation," Daniel said.

Chapter 9

The Akitu Festival

Judith's best friend in the entire Plain was Leah, the family cook. Whenever Judith had nothing better to do, she would head to the kitchen, where she would watch and even help Leah prepare a meal. During the three years that Leah had been with the family she had turned Judith from an indifferent eater into an underage gourmand who was willing to try anything at least once. Leah's success was attributed to her remarkable ability to transform the ordinary into the extraordinary, causing Judith to swoon and collapse onto a chair in pure ecstasy.

"*C'est magnifique*," Judith said after taking a bite of the fruit bar Leah had given her. "This is *absolutely* delicious."

"Then you approve?"

"Approve?" she said. "This is the best fruit bar ever created. How did you do it, Leah? Show me. I must learn how to make it."

Leah smiled, pleased. "Maybe tomorrow," she said. "Today I must prepare *kada* for the afternoon festivities. Would you like to help?"

"Yes, of course," Judith said, leaping from her chair to her feet. "Where do I begin?"

Judith could be either all boy or all girl, depending on the activity. In the kitchen today, working alongside Leah, Judith was all girl; her long black hair, which normally fell freely below her shoulders, was pulled together severely and tied near the skull with a ribbon. The rest of the hair fell behind her head in a well-groomed ponytail.

She stood on a box which her father had built for her to lift her high enough to work with ease at the table near Leah. The *kada* dough that Judith was trying to roll flat was being particularly belligerent. It refused to lay flat, insisting on sticking to everything – the roller, the board, and even her. For some reason, which totally baffled Judith, she was unable to stretch it effortlessly into a thin sheet. "Leah," she cried out in frustration, "what am I going to do? This dough is behaving *most* uncooperatively."

Leah, a large-figured woman of "some years," wobbled toward Judith. "Flour, Judith," she said. "You need more flour."

"Impossible!" Judith declared. "I have already used plenty."

Leah demonstrated her point after removing the dough from the rolling pin, the table, and Judith's fingers. She then shaped it into a disk. "Now watch me carefully." She sprinkled flour on the work table, the dough, and the rolling pin, then quickly and easily rolled the dough into a thin round sheet. "See, it's simple when you remember to sprinkle everything with flour." She placed another disk of dough on the floured table. "Here's another tip. Always roll from the center of the disk and work out, applying *even* pressure to the pin." She handed the rolling pin to Judith. "Now try again."

Judith followed Leah's instructions exactly. She stood on her toes, leaned forward over the table and applied even pressure to the rolling pin, as instructed. At the precise moment when she was leaning precariously forward, stretching the dough to its furthest limit, her mother entered the kitchen.

"Judith Shamash," she said in a halting voice. "Have you forgotten already?"

Startled, the girl pushed away the wooden box that she was standing on, lost her balance, and fell on the floor, taking with her a sack of flour. She emerged covered with flour.

"*Oh là là*. Look at you," her mother declared. "You're a mess. It will take forever to clean you up again." She extended a hand to Judith. "Come. We've got to hurry. We don't have much time to get ready."

"But I don't want to go. I want to remain here with Leah. May I, Mamma, *please*?"

Her mother stood firm; she was obviously not in the mood to deal with resistance. "That's very nice of you, Judith," she said. "But you'll just have to do that another time. Now we must get ready for *Akitu*."

Judith knew from her mother's inflexible tone that there was nothing further to say on the subject; she frowned as she obediently left with her mother.

Judith had always looked forward to *Akitu*. It was scheduled once a year to celebrate the cutting of the barley. Rooted in Assyrian history, this festival stretched back to the time of the ancient Babylonians. During the festivities, at least as celebrated by the Shamash family and their friends, everyone dressed in Assyrian costume, and they spent the day eating, dancing, and singing.

This year, though, her parents were breaking tradition; instead of attending their own festivities in their village, they were going to celebrate the festivities with the Oshanas.

"Remember," her mother said while dressing Judith. "I want you to be at your very best today. No wrestling with the animals or splashing in the water. In other words, I want you to behave like a young lady. Is that understood?"

"Yes, Mother," she said obediently.

Judith wondered how long it would take for her to forget her promise. What fun was a festival if she couldn't play with the animals or run through the garden, picking spring flowers? The thought of spending the day sitting with her ankles crossed, smiling politely on cue at all the old men and women who told her how sweet and cute she was, was unbearable, as unbearable as the thought of afternoon tea with the family.

No, she wasn't happy at all about attending the festivities at the Oshana village – not when she could be spending her morning preparing *kada* with Leah. At least if she stayed home and attended the festivities in her village, she would be free to enjoy herself without worrying about making a positive impression on strangers. But her mother insisted, leaving Judith with no choice but to cave in to her mother's will.

"Now step back," Abigail said after Judith was dressed. "Let me look at you."

Judith took several giant steps backwards. Her mother tilted her head to one side, and shook it. Something about Judith's appearance obviously didn't please her. She straightened her daughter's head-piece – rows of loosely connected silver coins that danced and jingled whenever Judith moved.

"Nope," she said. "That's not the problem."

Her gaze traveled over Judith's long white dress, embroidered with crimson crosses on each sleeve, and came to a halt at her waist. "That's the problem." Judith looked down to see what distressed her mother. Before Judith could ask her, Abigail removed a belt of silver coins from her table and wrapped it around Judith's waist. "Much better," she smiled. "Perfect. It shows off your small waist and it fluffs you up a little at the top." She turned her daughter around to face the mirror. "What do you think? Do you like how you look in your new dress?"

Given all the personal attention from her mother, Judith suspected that it was going to be a long, *boring* day. "It's okay," she said, wondering what horror awaited her at the Oshana's home.

Abigail responded cheerfully in an attempt to evoke enthusiasm. "Wipe away the gloom, *mon ange*, it won't be *that* bad. You are going to have a *wonderful* time, I guarantee. There will be many children your age there, including a few older ones – like Kushi."

"Who's that?"

"That's the Oshana's older son, so be nice to him. I want the family to like you."

Boring, she thought, wrinkling her face into a disagreeable frown.

"You mustn't frown," her mother said. "It betrays your thoughts."

Judith forced a broad smile; she then changed the subject before she could be asked to make promises that she might not want to keep, and she turned her attention to her mother, who was wearing a white tunic with crimson trim. A gold crown sat low on Abigail's head. Rubies, shaped to resemble pomegranates, hung loosely from the crown and danced over her forehead whenever she moved. In costume, her mother looked like a classic female beauty, a Babylonian goddess from history books – tall, graceful, and aristocratic. It was a look that Judith hoped she would inherit one day.

"You really look beautiful, Mamma," she said sincerely.

Her mother smiled, pleased. "Why thank you, Judith," she replied. "It's very kind of you to say that."

Malko entered the room and, when his eyes caught sight of his wife, his manly reserve immediately broke. "Wow," he said, his gaze surveying her. "You look magnificent!"

Smiling, Abigail made a gentle curtsy. "Thank you, my dear," she said. "And you, my Assyrian lord, look quite fetching too."

Judith was startled at the sight of her father in costume. He looked exactly like the Assyrian deity carved on her grandmother's brooch. He wore the same conical headdress, the same full-length tunic, and he even had his neck hidden by the same long and thick beard, combed straight and cut evenly at the ends. For a moment, it appeared to Judith as though the god carved in lapis lazuli had come to life.

"Daddy, you look just like that god carved on Grandmamma's brooch."

"I should. We have the same name."

"You mean Shamash, the sun god?" He nodded. "See, Daddy, you are wrong. We are descendants of gods. That's why you look like one in costume."

During the boat trip on the Shahar River to the Oshana village, Judith leaned over the edge of the railing and watched the activity on shore. In the fields, she saw the oxen-driven plows prepare the land for sowing. By the shore, several women wearing dark dresses and headscarves were washing clothes. The others were near a well; they were removing the copper containers strapped to their backs. After filling them with water, the women placed the containers on their shoulders and carried them back to the village.

Judith waved and called out *"shlama loukh,"* peace be with you, to the women washing their clothes. One woman looked up and waved back, while the others simply ignored her and continued with their duties. She turned to her mother standing beside her. "Is that the village where you and Auntie Suzy go each week?"

"One of them," her mother said.

"Do you help with the washing too?"

Abigail smiled, amused. "No, *chérie,*" she said. "I talk to them about the Lord, while your Auntie Suzy tends to the sick." Abigail then went on to explain how important her service was to the women. "Their husbands have no interest in their health or well-being, and they often treat them like slaves."

Judith listened thoughtfully while watching the women perform their daily duties. "Is that why they look so unhappy?"

"That's one reason," Abigail replied. "The other is that Mohammedanism doesn't offer them the same hope of eternal happiness as Christianity does."

"Why don't they leave and become Christians like us?"

"They wouldn't dare. They would be punished for disgracing their husbands. Not all those women are as courageous as Leah."

"Leah was a Mohammedan?" Judith asked, shocked.

"That's right. Many of the women working in Christian homes are just like Leah. They were once Mohammedans who gave their hearts to the Lord and who now support themselves by working in Christian villages."

"Why didn't Leah tell me?" Judith said, upset. "We're good friends. Good friends share secrets like that."

"Maybe it's because she didn't feel you would understand."

"But I would, Mamma. Honest."

"I know, dear, but maybe Leah doesn't."

"Can't something be done to free those other women too?" Judith asked, concerned.

"We are trying, but it is difficult. We are limited in what we can do by Sharia Law. So whatever we do we must do discretely. If their husbands ever found out, they would severely punish their wives, and God only knows what they would do to us. Such men consider women mere animals without any rights, pieces of property, whose life depends on the men's goodwill."

"That's *awful*, Mamma."

"Not in the eyes of Mohammedans."

"When I get home," Judith said, "I'm going to give Leah a big hug."

"I think she'd like that very much."

The Oshanas lived in a three-story stone house with a large front porch, lined with Corinthian columns, overlooking the garden. In terms of design, the house wasn't very different from her home. Like hers, it too had a twenty-foot high wall around it and heavy wooden doors with an iron knocker to summon the gatekeeper when closed. Today the huge doors were open, and the music beckoned the Shamash family into the garden where they were immediately seduced by the pleasant aroma of roses.

In the center of the garden was a large fountain with geometrically arranged ceramic tiles in varying shades of blue and white. Within each geometric design were crosses in a subtly darker shade of blue. Bright red rose petals floated in the fountain, kept in motion by the many bare feet splashing around in the shallow waters. Judith immediately wanted to kick off her shoes and join the other children playing in the water, but she knew better. She had made a promise to her mother to behave.

Near the fountain, the older guests were watching and clapping as men in baggy pants and embroidered jackets danced hand-in-hand with women in colorful tunics and silver- or gold-coin headpieces, shaking their bodies using lots of shoulder, foot, and arm movement, in time to the music.

Yusuf and Yasmine Oshana were the first to greet the Shamash family. They were a serene and gentle couple, very Patrician, about the same age as Judith's parents, with prominent noses and curly black hair.

After the two families exchanged their polite comments and Abigail presented Yasmine with a little gift, Yasmine turned to Judith. "You must be Judith. I recognize you from your picture in the *Bulletin*."

"Wasn't that some lucky discovery I made?" Judith said proudly.

"Very impressive," Yasmine said. "It isn't everyday that someone makes a discovery like that in the Plain."

"My granddaddy said the same thing. He thinks it could make me famous." Judith beamed with delight. "He thinks it could even get me mentioned in history books."

"He may be right," Yasmine smiled. "Your discovery confirms what historians have long believed. It clarifies the true antiquity of the Plain once and for all."

Judith felt herself swell with pride, almost to the point of bursting. Her mother turned to Judith before she could explode. "Why don't you enjoy yourself, Judith? Join the children next to the storyteller. We adults want to talk and catch up on local gossip."

Judith curtsied to the Oshanas, then hurried towards the others her age who were sitting on pillows in front of the storyteller. The young teenagers were listening to him tell a mesmerizing tale about the creation, skillfully weaved with enough mystery to make it exciting. En route towards them, she saw several children run past her carrying a collection of garden flowers and herbs to give to the men who used them to decorate the sides of the portico.

"Hello, Judith," a voice greeted her from under a shaded fruit tree. She turned towards the voice, but the sun was in her eyes, temporarily blinding her. All she could see was the silhouette of a man sitting in a chair. "Come and say hello," the voice beckoned.

Curious, she walked towards the voice. She immediately smiled when she recognized the Governor. His wickedly seductive blue eyes and his handsome smile beguiled her. "It is so nice to see you again, Sardar Jamshid."

"And it is nice to see you again too, Judith," he said, smiling. "My, you look pretty today." He made a circle with his finger. "Turn around, let me get a full view of you in your new dress." She spun around on her toes, making a full circle. "You're perfect," he said. "*Absolutely* perfect."

"My mother had the dress made especially for me to wear today. She wanted me to be particularly attractive for *Akitu*."

"You tell your mother she has succeeded," he said. "Come, sit next to me. Tell me what you've been doing lately."

"I'd like to, but I can't right now."

"Why not?" he said, frowning as though he were deeply hurt. "Don't you like me?"

It was a harmless question, yet Judith felt embarrassed by it. She backed away from him. "Of course, I like you," she said, blushing.

"Show me," he said, "Sit here next to me and talk to me for a few minutes."

"Maybe later," she said.

And before he could weaken her resistance with his devilish good looks, she curtsied and hurried away, breaking any connection he was trying to create between them. In her haste to join the cluster of teen-agers gathered around the storyteller, she collided with a boy a few years older than she. He was tall and thin, wiry in appearance, with long, dangling arms.

"Watch where you're going," he said, annoyed, when their bodies touched.

"I'm sorry," she said politely. "I didn't see you."

"If you had kept your eyes open, you would've," he said, standing very straight and proud, a peacock flashing his plumage. "As you can clearly see, I am not invisible."

She was startled by his response. It was obvious from the fuzzy black hair on his face that he was growing a mustache and a beard in order to appear older than he was. It was a pity, she thought, that he wasn't trying to learn good manners as well. "You're a very rude boy," she snapped. "I said I'm sorry. What more do I need to say to please your vanity?"

He was obviously offended by her audacity. She could tell by his startled reaction that no one had ever dared to speak to him that frankly before. After recovering from the shock, he was about ready to say something out of anger, but hesitated and studied her carefully. "You're Judith Shamash, aren't you?"

"That's right," she said cautiously, wondering who he was.

"You know, I was actually dreading meeting you." He cocked his head to examine her. "But I must admit you're prettier and older than you are in your newspaper photograph."

She held her head high like a Russian princess and eyed him sharply. "Is that supposed to be your way of apologizing for your bad manners?"

He was immediately amused. Her cutting remark shattered his arrogance and reduced him to the courteous gentlemen she was sure he was taught to be. "Yes, Miss Shamash, it is – in my obviously clumsy way," he added politely. "To avoid any further misunderstanding and to clarify my feelings, I want you to know that I think you are a very attractive young lady."

His unexpected attempt to be gallant surprised her, but it wasn't sufficient to eliminate the annoyance his earlier comments had caused her. "Thank you," she said coolly. "Now who are you?"

"I am Kushi Oshana," he said, "your future husband."

"My what?" she asked, shocked.

"Your future husband." He seemed to derive a boyish pleasure out of his remark.

She was horrified. *"Whatever* gave you that idea?"

"I overheard my parents discuss you the other day," he said. "That's why they've invited you here. They want to look you over and see if you are suitable."

"Well, as they have already discovered," she said, offended, "I am *quite* suitable, and, for the record, I am not interested in marrying you."

"Good," he said.

He did it again. He insulted me, she thought. She wanted to kick him hard in the leg, teach him a lesson, but once again she remembered her promise to her mother. "What's wrong?" she said. "Don't you think I am good enough to be an Oshana?"

"Of course you are. Very much so. In fact, you'd be a prize for any man," he said. "But I am going off to America next month to study, and I refuse to get married for a long time – regardless of what my mother and father may want."

"Well, I guess it works out well for both of us." She then walked away from him in the direction of the storyteller.

He ran in front of her and stopped her by extending his arm, which was too long for her to dodge. "Then it's official? You don't want to marry me?"

"That's right," she said. "Be assured. *It's official.*"

He then took her hand. She tried to pull herself free as he guided her away from the crowd, but he was too strong and insistent for her to succeed. "Come with me. Let's go somewhere private where we can talk and figure out together how to sabotage our parents' plans."

En route to a private hideaway, he grabbed a basket of food from the table and took it with him. Surrounded by aromatic flowers in bloom, they sat together in a small isolated clearing.

"Are you really sure our parents want us to get married?"

"That's what I overheard. My mother said your parents have been looking for the right husband for you for some time, someone suitable who can take care of you."

"You mean someone like *you?*" she said, horrified.

He was stunned by her statement. "Why not me?" he said defensively. "I come from an old Assyrian family. I will inherit lots of money. And, if I must say so," he raised his head high like a peacock, displaying his plume. "I am quite handsome."

"Wow!" she said. "You really have a high opinion of yourself."

"Don't you think I'm handsome?"

She hesitated. She wanted to say yes, because he was handsome. But she was wise enough to know that it would only feed his vanity, which would make him unbearable to be around. "Tell me, Kushi, how do you propose we sabotage their plan?"

"Simple," he said. "I have the perfect solution. Our parents don't know we know about their plans. So if we both convince them from the start that we don't like each other, we should be able to bring an end to this idea."

She looked at him, unimpressed. "Yes, but what good will that do? They will only find someone else for us – and we both could end up with someone even less suitable." And then she said to the young man with the fuzzy beard, "You know, for a boy, you aren't very smart."

"What's that supposed to mean?" he said, hurt. "That you are smarter because you found some bone in your dad's orchard?"

"It wasn't *just* a bone!" she responded sharply. "It was a *Paleolithic* bone."

"Okay, okay. You made a big discovery. I apologize."

"That's better," she said. "You should do that more often."

He ignored the comment. "I suppose you plan to be an anthropologist one day?"

"I'm not sure," she said. "All I know is that I want to be famous. I want everyone to know who Judith Shamash is." She reached into the basket and helped herself to some nuts. "What about you? What are you going to be?"

"I'm going to be an explorer."

"You mean like Christopher Columbus?" she said, impressed.

The boy in him surfaced. In his expression she saw adventure, excitement, *new horizons*. "Yes, that's right – just like the great explorers."

She was delighted. "*How exciting!*"

"My father doesn't think so," he said. "He thinks I should go into business like him. But I don't want to do that. I want to see the world."

"That's what I plan to do too," she said.

"Really?" he said, smiling as he eyed her with what appeared to be a new appreciation. "Most girls don't want to travel."

"I don't know what other girls want, but I do know what I want. And traveling the world making great discoveries is *exactly* what I plan to do with my life." She ate the shelled walnuts one at a time. She was beginning to feel comfortable with him. "Why are your parents sending you to America?" she asked suddenly. "Don't they like it here?"

"It's my dad's idea. He's worried there will be a war in the Plain, and he thinks I'll be safer in America."

"That's what my parents think too." She sighed. "I wish they'd worry about something else for a change."

"They have cause to worry," he said as if sharing an important secret. "Did you hear about what happened near Mosul recently?"

"You mean to those Christians?"

"Then you heard."

"Yes," she said solemnly, "my grandfather delivered a sermon on that several Sundays ago."

"Well, my father verified it, and he said Mohamad's report was a hundred percent true. During a business trip to Constantinople, he learned that Demir Pasha was planning to head eastward into Persia – slaughtering Christians along the way."

She gasped. "That's horrible."

"That's why my parents are taking no chances. They are moving all their money out of the country and planning to leave the Plain as soon as possible."

"My daddy said something like that too," she said.

"Wouldn't it be nice if he sent you to school in America?" His gaze settled on her in a familiar way, which made her blush. "If he did," he added unexpectedly, "we could see each other all the time."

She lowered her gaze. "You embarrass me when you look at me like that."

"I didn't mean to."

She lifted her gaze shyly, stirred by the unfamiliar emotions that she was beginning to feel towards him. "You are a strange one, Kushi Oshana – one minute you want to get rid of me, the next minute you don't."

"That's because you confuse me with your beauty." He leaned towards her, his expression softening with affection.

"Can I kiss you?"

"No," she said emphatically. "It's improper." Despite her objection, she made no effort to pull away from him. She was beginning to feel helplessly attracted to him.

"Please," he said. "We're practically engaged, and I may not see you again for a long time. You don't want me to go to America without even a goodbye kiss, do you?"

"I'm sorry. Kissing you is out of the question," she said, less emphatically.

"Just a little kiss?" he insisted. "That's all."

"Very well," she yielded, charmed by his insistence. "But *just* a little one."

She tapped her cheek with her finger, then closed her eyes and waited for him to kiss it. Instead, he held her head still with both hands and gently caressed her lips. Without resistance, she submitted to him, lips against lips.

Chapter 10

The Bazaar in Urmia, Autumn

Abigail was deeply worried by the news from Turkey. The *Zahria-d-Bahra* and other newspapers were all reporting regularly that the Germans controlled Constantinople and were having bawdy drinking parties in public areas nightly. The official explanation, issued by the Turkish consulate, was that the Germans had come to modernize the Turkish army; the unofficial explanation, told to her by friends, was that the Germans had come to claim the Ottomans as vassals.

One writer for *Zahria-d-Bahra* argued that the German occupation of Constantinople was part of Kaiser's plan to extend his reach into Asia; another argued the Kaiser was preparing the Turks for a border attack against their long-time enemy, the Russians. Regardless of the actual reason for the bonding of the two countries, the general message was the same: the Turks and the Germans were up to something big.

Reading such news left Abigail deeply worried. She believed what was happening in Turkey could spill over the mountains into the Plain any moment.

Sometimes, to calm the fear which such news brought her, she would seek comfort in appropriate verses from the Bible. That worked for a while, until she heard her father's sermon about Mohamad's experience near Mosul.

She suspected that, with Germany as an ally, the Turks would gain the strength and the skill to extend their crimes against Christians to the Plain and turn it overnight into a graveyard, as they were doing with the many Christian villages in Turkey.

As she sat alone in her room, Abigail knew it was time for the family to make plans to leave. Breaking free of her roots in Persia wasn't going to be easy for her. There was so much here that mattered to her. In the Plain, surrounded by thousands of years of history, she felt a unique attachment to the land that could never be duplicated anywhere else in the world. This land, where her ancestors had lived and died, was the cradle of civilization with a long and important Christian history. She doubted she could ever leave all this and move on into the unknown without feeling profound regret.

Thinking about the severe emotional discomfort such a move would cause her made her nervous and irritable. Yet she knew she couldn't delay departure any longer. Horrible events were unfolding daily. For Judith's sake, the family had to start making plans to leave as soon as possible. Until Judith was suitably married, Judith would have to be Abigail's primary concern.

In her zeal to protect Judith, Abigail was often hard on her daughter. This usually left Abigail feeling guilty of overreacting to trivial things – like her daughter spilling tea on a new dress or chasing Sag around the house. Yet when Abigail really thought about it, she sincerely believed she was behaving reasonably as a mother. The girl needed discipline. A time would come when Judith would have to show adult self-control to survive. It was Abigail's responsibility to teach it to her.

Yet she should never forget that Judith was growing slowly into a very sensible and intelligent young lady. Some things needed to be ignored. "Remember, you weren't an angel at her age," Miriam often reminded Abigail when the latter was too hard on Judith. "But look at you now, my dear," Miriam said, softening her disapproval with a little motherly love, "you've become a fine young lady with a wonderful heart and lots of good sense."

In the midst of Abigail's solitude, the door flung open; her daughter and Sag burst into the room like a tropical storm. Startled, Abigail dropped the newspaper she was holding and turned towards the noise. When her gaze met Abigail's, Judith stopped, pivoted, and quickly left the room, closing the door and leaving Sag behind to whine. She then knocked gently on the door.

"Come in, *mon ange*," Abigail said. "It's okay. I know it's you."

Her daughter appeared genuinely remorseful for her bold entrance. "I'm sorry, Mother," Judith said, stepping into the room, her head bowed. "I forgot to knock."

"It's okay this time, but try to remember, please," Abigail said, easing her daughter's unhappiness with a gentle explanation. "It's not good manners to enter a room without knocking." She then added affectionately, "Now, come here. Tell me what was so urgent that you felt it necessary to startle your mother like that."

Judith recovered almost instantly. She was once again a carefree thirteen-year-old girl about to release the latest, most exciting news in her life. "Grandmamma wants to take me to Urmia. Can I go with her, Mamma? *Please*."

Abigail smiled. "What do you and grandmother plan to do in Urmia?"

"We're going shopping," Judith said excitedly. "Grandmamma wants to buy me a doll, and she wants me to go along with her to pick it out."

"Another doll?" Abigail asked, surprised. "How many do you need? You already have a room full of them."

"No, I don't, Mamma. Not like the one I want."

"And what kind is that?"

"One of those biblical dolls with a violet tunic and navy sash, and a white prayer shawl covering her head." She smiled proudly. "That's the kind I want."

"It sounds as though you've already selected one without seeing what is available. Are you sure you will find such a doll?"

"Grandmamma says she knows exactly where to go to get one just like that."

"I am sure she does," Abigail said. "Your grandmother knows every bazaar in the Plain."

"So can I go, Mamma? *Please!*"

"Under one condition."

"Anything, Mamma. Anything."

"Promise me you will tell your grandmother that she can only buy you *one* doll, no more. Is that clear, Judith?"

"Yes, Mamma, that's clear." Judith threw her arms around Abigail and hugged her.

"Thank you, Mamma."

Abigail held her a few extra moments to savor the pleasure of the hug before her daughter wiggled herself free.

As Abigail watched her leave with a lively skip, she began to worry once again. With the world on the brink of madness, was this the time to encourage her daughter to buy more dolls? Frugality and sensibility was what she should be encouraging, not foolish greed for more things. This would be the perfect time to teach Judith that we can't always have what we want.

"Judith," she called before her daughter left the room. Judith froze. Obviously expecting the worst, she turned slowly and faced her mother with a look of worry. Abigail hesitated at saying what she wanted to say. She quickly smiled to ease her daughter's discomfort and said, "Tell your grandmother, no treats. I don't want you stuffing yourself before dinner tonight. Promise?"

"Yes, Mamma," Judith said with a look of relief. "I promise." She then hurried from the room, leaving the door open behind her. Sag followed, wagging his tail.

"Judith," her mother called.

Judith peeked into the room. "Yes, Mother."

"The door."

"Sorry, Mother, I forgot." And she gently closed the door behind her.

Outside the bazaar, impoverished Darvish beggars were singing, urging shoppers to give them coins. Some of the beggars had long black hair and full beards and mustaches, others had uncombed graying hair. Their orange fez caps and their patchwork robes were weathered, but when they sang their melodic Hafiz poems for money no one noticed their poverty. People – including Judith's grandmother – paused, enchanted by the rich sonority of their voices, and generously dropped coins into their cups.

The Bible Doll Shop was located inside the sixteenth century brick bazaar built during the Safavid era. To reach the shop, Judith and her grandmother had to pass through a busy passageway guarded by two beggars holding cups. One of the beggars was blind, and the other had his right hand and his left leg chopped off – their punishment, her grandmother told her, for stealing. The sight of them upset Judith. Seeing them so poor and deformed made her cringe. She tried to wipe the memory from her mind and hurry along with her grandmother, but she found it difficult. Their pitiful pleas for money and their desperate circumstances lingered on in her mind.

As Miriam led Judith through the bazaar, past all the shops lined next to each other, overflowing with merchandise that spilled into the busy passageway, a hawker stepped out of the crowd and blocked them. "Let me show you my beautiful new dresses. I've got all kinds, perfect for the young lady. Come inside. Let me show them to you. You'll love them. The best in Urmia, and at fair prices."

"I'm sorry," Miriam said, "not today."

"I insist. We can talk and have a little chai together. You will find I am good company."

"That's very kind, but we are in a hurry," Miriam said, and she walked around him, pulling Judith's hand. "Maybe later."

An Oriental rug dealer was standing outside his shop in front of columns of rolled rugs. When he caught Judith's eye, he bowed gently and made a sweeping gesture with his left hand, graciously inviting her and her grandmother into his shop. Miriam merely smiled politely, shook her head, and continued to lead Judith by the hand toward the Bible Doll Shop.

Ahead, a beam of light streamed through the ceiling skylight of the enclosed bazaar. It hit the display window of the doll shop like a spotlight and illuminated its content. Judith ran ahead of her grandmother when she saw the shop and responded with delight at the sight of the many dolls in the window. Unlike so many other shops in the bazaar, which filled their display space with a confusing selection of merchandise, the Bible Doll Shop arranged its merchandise neatly and carefully, so that each doll could be seen and appreciated. Some were even arranged around a special setting, which depicted the story associated with the doll. There was one with Moses standing on Mt Sinai, holding the Tablets of Law in his arms; another of Noah watching pairs of animals board the Ark; and still another of the Last Supper in which Jesus and his twelve disciples were sharing wine and bread together. Suspended from the ceiling on a string were more dolls, dressed like angels, watching over all the other dolls.

As Judith studied the beautifully created dolls, she wondered how she would ever make a decision.

"Do you see anything you like?" her grandmother asked.

Judith pressed her face against the glass to get a closer look. "Oh, Grandmamma, I love them all."

"I'm sure you do, Judith. But you can only have one. So which one will it be?"

"I don't know," she said very seriously. "They're all so special."

"Let's go inside and examine them closely. Maybe then it won't be so difficult to make a decision."

Judith was dazzled by all the beautiful dolls surrounding her in the shop. Seeing them all neatly displayed on shelves, in glass containers, and hanging suspended on a string from the ceiling only made her task of choosing one more difficult. *If only I could have them all*, she thought, *that would solve my problem, and I wouldn't have to choose.*

The merchant who approached them looked as though he had stepped from the pages of the Bible. He had a grey beard long enough to comb, and he wore a brown tunic and sandals. At first glance, he looked like a shepherd without a staff. After politely greeting him, Judith gave no further attention to him. She was more interested in his doll collection.

Which one do I want? she asked herself. The one she thought she wanted was no longer of interest. There were too many other dolls, more beautiful. There were the three wise men, carrying gifts to baby Jesus; the Israelite blowing the trumpet that brought down the walls of Jericho; and Joseph wearing his coat of many colors. But of them all, the one which she fell in love with the moment she saw it was the Queen of Sheba. It was the most beautiful and delicate-looking doll she had ever seen. The details of its porcelain face were so exact that Judith had to touch it to be sure it was a doll, not a miniature human in jewels and an embroidered dress.

"This is the one I want, Grandmamma," Judith said, holding the doll for her grandmother to see. "Isn't she the most beautiful doll you've ever seen?"

Her grandmother smiled, pleased. "Yes, you are absolutely right. She certainly is." She then asked

Judith, before finalizing the sale, "Are you *absolutely* sure this is the one you want?"

"Oh yes, Grandmamma," Judith said. "She's perfect."

"Then it's settled," Miriam said. She then turned to the merchant. "One Queen of Sheba for my little queen."

"Grandmamma, is it possible...?" Judith turned her most adorable smile on, the one which she reserved for those moments when she wanted something really special.

Her grandmother looked at her curiously. "What is it, my dear?"

"Could I possibly get King Solomon too?" she asked in her sweetest voice. "The two dolls belong together, don't you think?"

"Have you already forgotten your promise to your mother?"

"Can't we tell her they're a pair and you had to buy both?"

"That would be lying."

"But they are a pair," she said, trying to justify her request.

Her grandmother hesitated. Judith turned her adorable smile into an adorable pout and watched her grandmother quickly melt. "Okay, but you must agree to something first," Miriam said.

"Anything, Grandmamma, I promise," Judith said unhesitatingly. Afterwards, she wondered if she should have agreed so quickly without first hearing the terms.

"Here's my condition. I'll give you one doll right away and the other one for Christmas. Is that acceptable?"

"Oh yes, Grandmamma. Indeed, that's quite acceptable." She then thought for a moment, tugged on her grandmother's sleeve. "You know, of course, Christmas won't be for a while. Is it possible for me to play with the other doll once in a while before then?"

"Absolutely not," Miriam said. "The agreement must be: you get one doll now and the other one for Christmas."

Judith frowned, but only briefly. She got what she wanted – even if it meant she would have to wait a while before she could enjoy her gift.

Miriam turned to the merchant and asked him to wrap King Solomon, while Judith held on to the Queen of Sheba. As her grandmother talked to the merchant who was wrapping the doll, Judith wandered about the store examining the displays.

After the dolls were paid for and King Solomon was wrapped, Miriam turned to get Judith. But to her surprise, Judith wasn't anywhere in sight.

"Judith," she called out. There was no answer. She was frantic. "Judith, where are you?"

"She left with her father a few minutes ago," the merchant said.

"You must be mistaken," she said, confused. "Why would you say that?"

"I saw her talking to a distinguished-looking man in western clothes, and I just assumed he was her father when they left hand-in-hand."

Everything suddenly seemed unreal, beyond belief. One minute she was talking to her grandchild and the next minute Judith was gone. "Oh, dear God," she said. "Someone stole my precious baby. Oh tell me, God, that I'm wrong!"

"I swear, madam," he said. "I saw it while I was wrapping the doll."

She ran from the shop in panic. "Judith," she cried out. "Judith, where are you?"

But her voice could not carry above all the noise in the bazaar. The passageway was filled with too many shoppers, all talking at once. Miriam pushed her way through the crowd. Everywhere she went she stopped people and frantically asked them the same question. "Have you seen my grandchild? She's about four feet tall, wearing a blue coat and a red scarf, with a bow in her hair?"

One man said he saw someone who fitted her description with a man in a business suit. He pointed toward the exit. "They went in that direction."

Miriam hurried from the bazaar. When she was outside, she looked up and down the street for some sign of Judith. But she saw no one resembling her granddaughter. "Judith," she cried out in tears, "Where are you?"

People stopped and asked her what was wrong. "My grandchild," she said. "I'm looking for my grandchild." She then asked them the same question. "Have you seen her? She's a thirteen-year-old girl wearing a blue coat and a red scarf." No one could provide any information.

Maybe she wasn't kidnapped. Maybe Malko met her. But why didn't he say something to her? No, Malko would never have been that thoughtless. It had to be someone from church. That's got to be it. But if he was from church, why didn't he speak to her? No, impossible. No one she knew would ever do something like that. The only explanation that made sense was that Judith was kidnapped. Horrible stories of Christian girls being stolen and sold into slavery came to mind.

Her gaze drifted around the area in search of some clue – something that would provide her with a hint of where Judith might be. Then, she saw it. Covered with dust, it was lying on the street – the Queen of Sheba.

Abigail glared at her mother, untouched by her sorrow, totally unsympathetic to her remorse. She was a stereotypical mother in shock over losing her child, a mother beyond reason, a mother too upset to understand anything except the personal pain she was feeling at that moment. "How could you be so careless?" Abigail said to Miriam. "You know what a free spirit she is."

"But it happened so quickly," Miriam said in defense. "One minute she was there. The next minute she was gone." She collapsed into the chair, covered her face with her hands, and silently wept.

"I'll never forgive you for this, mother," Abigail said. "*Never!*"

Miriam looked up at her tearfully, her expression begging for forgiveness. "You don't understand, Abigail. There wasn't anything I could've done to prevent it. One minute I was negotiating the price for the dolls, and the next..."

"Dolls," Abigail said. "You bought her *dolls*? I specifically said ONE doll, mother."

"I know, but she saw this pair, and I thought I would give her one now and the other for Christmas."

"You always have an excuse for ignoring my requests."

"But I..."

Abigail silenced her with a freezing stare.

Why did I ever let her go shopping? she kept asking herself. *I should've put my foot down and said "Absolutely not. No more dolls for you, young lady. You have enough." But I didn't. And because I didn't, at this very moment some man is probably fondling her. God only knows to what limits he will go for his pleasure. How could I have been so foolish to entrust my mother with Judith, knowing how easily Judith could manipulate her?*

Abigail remembered how she used to push her mother to the limit when she was Judith's age. Nothing could stop Abigail when she wanted something. And now her daughter was doing the same thing, and, as a result, Judith had placed herself in a situation in which she could be disgraced for life.

Malko was in the stables, removing the saddle from his horse, when he saw Abigail approach. He immediately reacted with concern at the sight of her. This was one of the rare moments in her life when Abigail didn't artfully conceal her feelings behind a veneer of reserve. A raw look of pure sorrow covered her face. In all their years together, he had never seen her reveal so much of herself in one moment.

She didn't say anything immediately when she reached him. She just collapsed into his arms and clung tightly to him. Only once in her life had she displayed a profound need for him – and that was after Dakan had left for America. Like then, she now sought from him what she needed the most – his strength.

"What is it, honey?" he asked.

"It's Judith."

His heartbeat stopped. "What about Judith?"

"She's gone."

Alarmed, he turned her head up towards his. "What do you mean, *gone*?"

"She's been kidnapped, Malko," she was crying. "Someone took our little girl."

With just those few words, she had successfully pierced his shield and fatally wounded him. He was no longer the mighty Assyrian warrior who could match his strength against anyone. Instead, he was a broken man, Samson without his locks.

Chapter 11

The Urmia Plain

Haamid interrupted the conversation to light his kalian. He did it in a leisurely way, with elegant ease, like a master who took pride in his skill. After he struck the flint and steel together to ignite the tender, he used the fire to light his water pipe. Once it was lit, he inhaled deeply; smiling contentedly, he relaxed in his chair as though this was the most enjoyable moment of his life. While Haamid contentedly exhaled the smoke, Haron anxiously waited for him to continue with the conversation.

"Now where was I?" Haamid asked.

Haron responded immediately, annoyed by his delays. "You were telling me about the latest report from Turkey."

Haamid took a leisurely sip of his hot tea. "That's right. I almost forgot." He then set his tea glass on the saucer before placing it on the table. As he was just about ready to continue, he sneezed, not once but several times in rapid succession. His entire body responded, resulting in what appeared to be uncontrolled, spasmodic fits, which lasted almost a minute. "God be praised," Haamid said after he had recovered.

Haron courteously replied to his Mohammedan companion, "God have mercy on you."

Haamid smiled politely at Haron before continuing. "As I was saying," he said, pausing just long enough to have another sip of tea, "it won't be long before the inevitable occurs."

Haron became frightened. "You mean war?"

"Exactly, my friend. The Young Turks are very ambitious, and they are set on conquering Persia."

"Impossible! The Russians would never permit it."

"I wouldn't count on that," Haamid said. "I heard rumors the Turks have plans for them too."

Haron was uncomfortable with the subject, but, like all Christian men with families, he needed answers. He was worried about what could happen to him and his family if the Turks did successfully invade Persia. He set his tea glass down, spilling some on the saucer.

"What kind of plans?"

Several Mohammedan men entered the teahouse; they were followed by their wives, who were covered in black cloth. Haron glanced at them briefly, just long enough to see them enter. His full attention remained on his pipe-smoking friend.

Haamid slowly released the smoke drawn through the serpentine stem of his water pipe. "My sources weren't explicit," he said.

"That may be because they don't know," Haron said. "How could the Turks ever attack Persia? They haven't recovered from the Balkan wars. To fight both the Russians and the Persians, they would have to have enormous resources."

"Haven't you been reading the newspapers? The Germans are training them." Haamid then leaned forward and said confidentially, "If I may make a suggestion, I think you and your family ought to leave the Plain as soon as possible. As Christians, you face serious dangers here."

"We can't leave. We have no place to go."

"You can't stay here, that's for sure. Who will protect you?"

As the two men talked, a man entered the café, breathless. He hurried to a table where several men were sitting. "It's happened," he said, loud enough for everyone to overhear. "The Turks destroyed the Russian naval fleet in the Black Sea."

Shocked silence settled in the café. For several moments, no one spoke. A single, terrified and trembling voice broke the silence. "Are you sure?" Haron asked. "Are you really sure?"

"It just came by telegraph," the man announced. "The *Goeben* and the *Breslau* have destroyed the ports of Novorossiysk, Odessa and Sevastopol."

"The *Goeben* and the *Breslau*?" Haron asked.

"The two warships Germany gave to the Turks."

"Then it is true."

"I'm afraid so. The Turks have joined forces with the Central Powers and declared war on Russia."

Everyone in the teahouse began to talk at once. The subject was the same. "What is going to happen next? Would the Turks attack the Russians in the Caucasus? What will happen to the Armenians – and the Assyrians – in the Plain?"

The big, overriding question that concerned Haron was: What should he do? There was nowhere to run. Russia was the only immediate exit, but how safe would Russia be, and for how long, if defeated by the Turks?

"America," someone shouted, answering the question for him. "There is always America."

"Yes, but how do we get there? What road do we take to freedom if the entire Europe is at war?"

"We are walled in," one Assyrian man said sadly. "Our only hope is to join the Russians and fight our way to freedom."

"Have you forgotten what the Sultan did to the Armenians in the '90s when they took sides with the Russians?" another man said. "Do you think the Young Turks will be kinder?"

"What's our choice?" Haron asked.

"We have no choice," the Assyrian man said.

Haron turned white with fear. He excused himself and hurried from the café.

Miriam Tamras panicked when she heard the news that the Turks had declared war against the Russians. Whatever hope she had nurtured of finding her granddaughter was crushed. If war came to the Plain, as everyone suspected, it would bring with it so much confusion that it would make it impossible to find Judith again. Everyone would be so busy scrambling for safety that any evidence that might exist of her granddaughter's whereabouts would be lost in the confusion. If Judith were to be found at all, she would have to be found now – before the Plain became a war zone. Desperate for a solid lead, Miriam returned to the bazaar. Maybe today she would meet someone who would have news to share about Judith's disappearance.

When she arrived at the bazaar, everyone was talking about the Turks' attack on Russian ports. It was almost impossible to get anyone's attention. When Miriam succeeded, they would listen sympathetically, offer a few kind words, and quickly return to their discussion of the war. Her inability to maintain their interest for any length of time confirmed how difficult searching for her granddaughter was going to be now

Discouraged, the only thing Miriam could do was to hand them one of Judith's pictures. "If you learn anything, please notify me," she said. "There will be a reward – a sizeable reward if she is found alive."

The merchant at the Bible Doll Shop had removed the dolls from his display window. He was wrapping them individually and placing them neatly in boxes when she entered his shop. The display areas, once lined with beautiful dolls, were empty. On the floor against the counters stood waist-high stacks of boxes.

"You are leaving?" she said to the gray-bearded man in the full-length tunic.

"Yes, it's time to leave. If the Turks attack, they will only destroy my shop. So I might as well depart while I have the chance."

"Is this how it'll be for us?" she said sadly. "Forced to wander the wilderness like the Israelites in search of the Promised Land?"

"For many, yes. The lucky ones, on the other hand, may find safety, maybe even peace, somewhere. But for the rest of us it may be time to prepare to meet our creator."

She stopped thinking about the war and refused to yield to fear. She stood firm and decisive, a pillar of strength that couldn't be intimidated by anything. "I am not ready to leave this earth. Not until I find my grandchild."

"You still haven't heard a word?"

"Nothing." She held back the tears, welling up within her, with the sheer strength of her will. "Not a single word."

He looked at her, an understanding father who wanted to comfort her with a few kind words. "She's been in my prayers for several days," he said. "Is there anything more you would like me to do?"

She handed him Judith's photo. "Maybe you can show this to your friends. Someone must know something."

As she left the bazaar, she wondered if Judith was being held captive in this very area at this very moment. Could she be locked up somewhere right under her nose? But where? There was no secret place in the area to hide a child, except in the back room of some small shop. The likelihood of someone doing that was remote. There was the probability that she might be discovered. Still, it was possible – at least for a short period.

But if this were the case, what kind of plans did her abductor have for her? If money was what he wanted, he would have certainly tried to contact the family by now. No, she thought, it wasn't a ransom he wanted. He had something else in mind.

But what could it be?

Stories of what depraved men did to young girls came to mind. These stories terrified Miriam, making it impossible for her to think clearly. To make matters worse, she couldn't shake away her guilt for contributing to Judith's disappearance. Why did she take her granddaughter to the Bible Doll Shop? She knew about Judith's passion for dolls. She knew how easily Judith could be tempted. If only Abigail wasn't so angry with her, if only her own daughter would just show a little forgiveness, it might make it easier to deal with the gnawing pain she felt whenever she thought about Judith.

As she stood outside the bazaar, surveying the area, her gaze settled on the spot where she found the Queen of Sheba doll, and she began to tremble. What could that evil man have promised Judith to get her to go with him willingly? For all her brightness, Judith was so innocent and vulnerable. If the family were fortunate enough to find her, would she still be the same child they all loved? Would she still beam with adorable innocence, or would the painful memory of her experience wipe it all away?

Who could be behind this terrible act? Who would have strong enough reason to kidnap her? Miriam thought of what loomed beyond the walls of the city, beyond the Plain, and focused on the Zagros Mountains. She stumbled away from the bazaar, like a drunk without balance or direction. "The Kurds," she said. "It had to be *them!*"

She lost control of herself and collapsed onto a chair at an outside café. She lowered her head and cried sorrowfully. No one seemed to notice her. They all seemed too busy talking about Turkey's declaration of war against Russia.

Abigail couldn't forgive Miriam for Judith's disappearance. Her anger with her mother gnawed at her, destroying Abigail's ability to be civil and reasonable. When her mother entered a room, Abigail would leave. If her mother asked her something, she would mumble a response and bury herself in whatever she was doing. Abigail knew that if she said anything to her mother, the words would be cruel.

I shouldn't have permitted her to take Judith shopping, she thought, torturing herself. *I should have put my foot down the moment the subject came up. But no, I foolishly softened and gave in to Judith. And I did it knowing how much her grandmother enjoyed spoiling her. It's unbelievable how deliberately my own mother defies my wishes. I tell her to buy Judith one doll and she buys her two. How could she do this to me? I will never be able to develop sound values in that girl if my very own mother continuously undermines my efforts with her extravagant gifts. It's her fault that girl is turning into such a willful and spoiled child. If she had more concern for Judith's well-being, mother would never pamper her so shamelessly. I will never forgive mother! Never!*

Yet she knew deep down, when reason melted her anger, that it wasn't her mother's fault. Miriam loved her grandchild as much as Abigail did. There was no evil intent in her actions. Like the rest of the family, she just found it difficult to resist Judith's charm. Judith had such a healthy passion for life, a *joie de vivre*, and when she dazzled one with her large almond eyes or her cute pout, it was impossible to resist her and say no.

Abigail had to face the facts. Even if Miriam were careful and kept a close watch on Judith, her daughter still could've been kidnapped. These were difficult times. No matter how protective her grandmother would have been, someone intent on kidnapping Judith would have found a way. War brought out the worst in people. Desperate for money, people were willing to do anything to survive.

She knew she must stop accusing her mother and start showing some compassion. When Abigail needed her after Dakan left for America, Miriam never probed for any explanation. Instead, her mother respected her silence and gave Abigail all the room she needed to deal with her problem alone. A watchful and caring mother, Miriam remained in the shadows, ready to assist Abigail in any appropriate way if it became necessary. Now the situation was reversed, and Abigail didn't even try to return her mother's kindness.

By blaming her mother for her daughter's disappearance, she was able to free herself of any blame and guilt. The truth of the matter was that Abigail was responsible for the kidnapping because she so stubbornly refused to leave the Plain and take her daughter to safety. If she had at least sent Judith to school in America, as the Oshanas had done with Kushi, her daughter might be safe now. Abigail knew the Plain was changing rapidly; one day it would become a war zone. Yet she had made no effort to protect Judith. She promised herself if her daughter returned safely, they would all leave Persia immediately. There would be no further delays.

But she mustn't think about that now. This wasn't the time to concern herself about what she should have done. This was the time to act. Her daughter had been kidnapped, and her responsibility now was to find her before a war broke out in Persia.

With her sister-in-law by her side, Abigail turned to their Mohammedan friends, seeking from them the support the two women so desperately needed. When Abigail showed a photo of Judith to one friend, sadness flashed across the friend's unveiled face, aging her. Abigail knew what Cantara was thinking. Cantara knew from personal experience how brutal men could be. During the course of their friendship, Cantara had told Suzy and Abigail many painful stories about the lustful and sadistic nature of her husband. But instead of reminding them about her own experiences and causing them further worry, Cantara gave them positive support. "She'll be all right," Cantara said. "Not all men are brutes like my husband. She'll come home soon. You'll see."

"But will she come home chaste?" Abigail said.

"Don't worry, Abigail. She'll be fine. From what you have told me about her, she'll figure out a way to protect herself. She sounds like a bright child, so stop worrying about her. I'll do what I can for you by spreading the word to my friends."

"Promise me, if you learn anything, *anything*, night or day," Abigail said with a note of desperation in her voice, "you'll contact me?"

"Of course. Immediately."

"Can you also ask your husband about her? He might know something that he could share with us."

"Don't count on that happening," Cantara said. "To him, women are mere servants, too stupid for respect. He couldn't care less what happens to them."

"Then listen when he speaks. Please listen to everything he says," Abigail said. "Maybe he will say something relevant that will help us find her. I worry every moment she's away. If we don't find her soon, she could be taken out of the country, or..." She couldn't finish the sentence or even the thought.

Cantara put her arms around Abigail and held her close against her strong body, a body made firm by hard labor and great suffering. "Stop thinking like that, Abigail," she said. "We'll find her. Somehow, together, we'll find her."

Daniel was tormented by the thought of something foul happening to his grandchild. Despite her spirited ways, which sometimes got her into trouble, he saw in her a promise of salvation for the Assyrians. One day her brightness would light up the world. She had a huge capacity for learning and the intelligence to solve problems quickly. She was a clever girl, a determined girl. Knowing she was gone, aware that some man might be violating her, maybe even torturing her with his shameless abuse, caused him a pain greater than he could bear.

Dear, beloved Father, Daniel prayed earnestly, *some things are beyond my powers to understand. Some things I must just leave in your hands. But I beg you with all my heart, please spare my grandchild. My life is nearly complete; let me give you what's left of it willingly. Take it if you must. Use it for your glory. All I ask in return is for you to deliver Judith to her parents safely. These are painful times for the family, and I can't bear to see them suffer. I beg you, dear Lord. Give us some peace.*

Malko didn't know where to turn. Silence surrounded Judith's disappearance. Because of his position in the province, he was normally able to obtain answers quickly. There was always someone who knew something, especially for a little gold. But now, when he really needed information, when he turned desperately to others for assistance, no one had anything to share. He wanted to publish something in *Zahria-d-Bahra* and alert everyone in the Plain to her disappearance, but he hesitated, fearful that it might force the kidnapper to act hastily and cover his trail. This could endanger his daughter's life. It was better, Malko believed, to work undercover – to find out about her privately by word of mouth. Eventually he would find someone who had something to share.

All he needed was a grain of information. That might be just enough to send him off searching in the right direction. The only lead he had so far was the Queen of Sheba doll found outside the bazaar. It was obviously dropped during her daughter's struggle with her captor. Normally, Malko was a man who knew no fear. He confronted adversity with acts of valor. But for the first time in his life he felt helpless. Without a clue to direct him, without a strong line of action to take, there was nothing he could do but wait. He was terrified.

This wasn't an ordinary kidnapping. Usually in cases like this, when they knew the family had money, they would try to arrange a ransom. A message would be sent, some whisper of hope would reach him through friends. If that had occurred, he would at least have something to deal with – a problem with a possibly negotiable solution. But the fact that he hadn't heard anything left him fearing that he was dealing with a horrendous crime that he couldn't stop.

Having nowhere to turn, surrounded by silence, Malko had only one choice: to seek the Governor's assistance. Like other Urmians, he didn't trust the Governor. Yet Malko still maintained his friendship.

The Governor had spies everywhere, watching over the community and secretly collecting information about everything important. Many of these spies traveled inconspicuously throughout the Plain, hiding their identity under the guise of friendship. If the Governor's spies couldn't uncover anything about his daughter's whereabouts, no one could.

Filled with ancient Persian artifacts and intricately designed Oriental rugs, the Governor's stone house was like a huge museum. It was a monument to corruption, built with stolen treasures and *baksheesh*. When dealing with the Governor, it was never wise to reveal the extent of one's wealth. Given the sheer power vested in him by the Royal Family in Teheran, the Governor could claim whatever he wanted from his subjects. A sword bestowed to him by the Shah hung on his reception room wall. It was placed there as a conspicuous reminder to anyone entering the Governor's home that he had the legal power to take what he wanted from them – including their lives, if necessary.

Malko knew that, so long as Persia wasn't at war with any major Christian countries (especially Russia and Britain), the Governor would have to behave judiciously towards the Christians and always show an attitude of cooperation.

"*Shlama loukh*," the Governor greeted him.

"Peace be with you, too," Malko replied politely.

"Have you heard anything about Judith?"

"You learned about her disappearance already?" Malko said, not surprised.

The Governor's servant poured some tea for the two men. "Everyone in the Plain knows about it," the Governor answered.

"Why hasn't someone come forth with some news, then? Could it be there's been foul play?"

"On the contrary, I think it's a good sign."

"Why would you say that?" Malko asked, confused.

"It's been my experience that bright girls like Judith leave home suddenly for a reason."

The Governor placed a lump of sugar in his mouth and dissolved it by drinking some hot tea, while observing Malko's reaction.

"What sort of reason?"

"Usually," he said confidently, "to convert to Mohammedanism."

"That's unlikely. Judith is a devout Christian."

"It may seem so to you. But to Judith Mohammedanism may be more appealing than Christianity. In the Koran, there is a great deal of wisdom which young girls can't find in the teachings of Christ." The Governor set his tea glass down, leaned back into his chair, and observed Malko's reaction. "Just recently, for example, in Tabriz," he said, pressing his point, "three young Christian girls voluntarily converted to the faith after secretly meeting with a mullah. Today, those same girls have married respectable Mohammedan men and are living quite devout lives. So, you see, it's very possible that the same thing could happen to Judith."

His explanation was preposterous, Malko thought. Did the Governor actually believe Malko would accept it? Was it possible that he knew something and was preparing Malko for what might follow? Malko decided to lead him on and see if he were correct.

"I know my daughter," Malko said. "Judith would never change her faith willingly."

Malko noticed a hint of amusement in the Governor's expression. It was playful, like that of a cat looking at a mouse before the kill. If Malko was right, he had to approach the Governor shrewdly, without revealing emotion. The Governor had a reason to make such an outrageously improbable statement. Either he knew something Malko didn't know, or he was just using this moment to get some *baksheesh*.

Malko discretely slipped him a small leather pouch with some gold coins in it. The Governor smiled when he heard the familiar jingle of coins. The pouch quickly disappeared into the Governor's pocket. "You realize, Malko, if I am correct, and she did voluntarily convert to Mohammedanism, returning her to you could be costly."

"I am sure of that," Malko said. "Still, if I could persuade you to use your vast influence to locate her, we could always address that financial issue later." Malko wondered how much gold the Governor would want in order to locate his daughter. He decided to test the matter and added diplomatically,

"I realize that a discreet search for my daughter will require a commitment from you and the police beyond your personal responsibility. With that in mind, I am quite willing to cover any expenses that you may incur while investigating her disappearance."

Greed flickered in the Governor's eyes and remained there long enough to reflect in his entire expression. "You know, of course, there's no guarantee I will succeed," he said. "There is the chance she may insist on following her new faith and refuse to return home."

"I will keep that in mind," Malko said.

"If that becomes the case, you may have to make a major financial contribution to her future."

"How major?"

"As you know, Islamic law can be very complicated, and it can sometimes be uncompromising. When a Christian girl converts to the Islamic faith, it isn't unusual for the family – especially a wealthy family like yours – to provide a generous inheritance for her to share with her mullah and her future husband."

"You mean they want my daughter and my money too?" he said, shocked.

"That's one way of putting it."

Malko had encountered his share of greed, but never anything like this. It was obvious the Governor was preparing him for a huge ransom, which obviously meant one thing: *he knew exactly where Judith was.*

Malko hid his contempt for the Governor and Sharia Law by feigning innocence. *This is a business deal*, he kept repeating to himself, *and I have to treat it as such, if I want Judith home safely.*

"Money isn't my primary concern," Malko said in his most diplomatic and polite voice. "Remember, Sardar Jamshid, we are dealing with my daughter, and I will obediently do whatever is necessary to ensure her safety and happiness."

"You are a very loving father indeed," the Governor smiled benevolently.

"And you are a very kind friend to want to assist me in locating her."

Chapter 12

The Bazaar in Urmia

Judith was looking at other dolls, while her grand-mother paid for the two dolls that she had selected. As she gazed with greedy interest at all the other dolls, Judith wondered if it would be prudent to ask her grandmother to buy her a third one. She was pondering this when a man wearing a pince-nez and a western suit entered the shop and approached her.

"Hello, Judith," the man said.

She looked up at the stranger, puzzled. *Did she know him?* If she did, she had no idea when or where they might have met. "Hello," she said politely.

"Your father told me to get you," the man said softly, as though sharing an important secret. He smiled handsomely, revealing a beautiful set of white teeth. "He has a surprise for you."

"Surprise!" she erupted with delight.

He quickly put his finger to his lips. "Not so loud," he said. "I'm not supposed to say anything. Your father wants it to be a surprise."

She lowered her voice and gushed excitedly, "What kind of surprise?"

"I can't tell you. It wouldn't be a surprise if I told you."

"Then give me a little hint," she begged. "Just a *tiny* one. That's all."

"Okay, but only a very tiny one," the man said, ingratiating her with his playful glance. "It's something you've always wanted."

"Hmmm, what can that be?" She tried to remember the long list of things she absolutely had to have, when a thought unexpectedly exploded in her head. "I know! It's a dollhouse. Of course, it's got to be a dollhouse. Daddy's been promising to build me one for ages."

"Better than that!"

She couldn't control herself. The thought of receiving a really special gift, one that she had always wanted, was just too exciting. But what could it be? Everything that came to mind was nice, but nothing was really special.

"Oh, tell me, please. I must know."

"I can't. I promised your father that I'd keep it a secret. You'll just have to come with me and find out for yourself."

"Okay," she said, "but I'll have to tell my grand-mamma first. She's right over there, talking to the salesman."

"No need for that. She already knows," he said. "Come, hurry. I don't want you to miss out on the fun."

He took her hand, holding onto it firmly, almost to the point of discomfort. Too excited to care, she gave in to the stranger and eagerly hurried from the shop. All the things she had ever wanted flowed through her mind, uninterrupted. *Which one could it be?* she kept asking herself. *Oh, I can't wait to find out.* They hurried through the bazaar hand-in-hand, breaking through the crowd ahead in what was almost a run. But when they left the bazaar, and he was leading her, faster than she could walk, towards a side street, she halted in her tracks.

Judith stared at the winding, quiet street ahead with alarm. A man wearing a jacket of many bright colors was blocking the narrow street with his ox-driven cart. "Where are we going?"

"Just down the street."

"I don't see anything there, just that man and his cart."

"He's going to take us to your father. Come, we're almost there."

Judith stood firm. The sight of the man by the cart frightened her. He was a big, strong man with wild-looking hair and a large knife attached to his belt. He resembled one of those mountain Kurds whom she had often heard about. She tried to break away from her escort, but he gave her a violent pull into the deserted street. Panicking, she deliberately dropped the Queen of Sheba.

"My doll," she said. "I dropped my doll."

"Forget it," he said. "I've got others for you, prettier ones."

"But I want my Queen of Sheba." She tried to break away from him, but he wouldn't let go and merely tightened his hold on her hand, pulling her closer to the cart. "Let go," she began to cry. "You're hurting me."

He stopped walking and turned to her. "If you don't shut up," he said in a cold, cruel voice, "I'm going to shove that doll into that pretty mouth of yours."

She was stunned by his tone, by the violent look of hatred on his face. The gentle man in the Bible Doll Shop had become a monster. Driven by fear, she began to push and pull, swing and kick at him with remarkable strength and effectiveness, which surprised him. When he was struggling to hold on to her, his glasses fell from his nose. Instead of letting go to retrieve them, as she had hoped, he merely signaled the man standing by the cart to come to his aid. In an act of fury, she stepped on the glasses and crushed them. Before she could start screaming in protest, she disappeared into a large sack. She was then lifted, while she kicked and punched the sack, and tossed onto a pile of straw in the cart.

"One more word out of you and I'll crush your skull with my foot," the man said in a voice as frightening as his threat. Terrified, she lay still on her straw bed.

The ride from Urmia through the Plain seemed to take forever. Her body bounced and rolled with each bump in the road. Why did she so stupidly trust this man and leave with him? She should've called her grandmother. That would've been the smart thing to do. But no, not for Judith. She had to yield to temptation and place herself at risk – without giving any consideration to the possible consequences. What was she going to do now? Even more frightening was, *what was he going to do?*

She listened keenly to the sounds around her, hopeful they might provide a clue to where she was heading. But all she heard while leaving Urmia were distant voices and the occasional bleats of sheep herded by barking dogs. It was early evening when the man removed the sack.

The cold, gray Zagros Mountains with their snow -capped peaks loomed before her. She was quickly led into a walled area within a small village. Ahead of her, behind a few fruit trees and rose bushes, was a house. Unlike her stone house, this one was a typical mud-brick one with a flat-roof. Like many such houses in villages, it was joined to the other houses at the roof to create a walkway for villagers to use when the streets were muddy.

Inside the house, there was an oven in which bread was being baked. Its pleasant aroma filled the room, mingling with the nauseating scent of vomit that slowly exited through an open skylight. To avoid regurgitating in the almost airless sick room, Judith began to swallow repeatedly.

Mats covered the dirt floor. Oriental rugs had been laid over the mats to create a bed in one corner. A woman dressed in black was sleeping there.

"Get up, *kahba*!" her kidnapper said to the woman contemptuously. "We want to eat."

The woman awakened, startled. Fear crossed her face. She lifted her body awkwardly, using both arms to rise to a sit-up position. She was pregnant and looked as though she would explode any moment.

"Damn you, woman. Move faster! I'm hungry," the man said unsympathetically.

Judith ran to the woman. Startled, the woman looked at the girl and thanked her when Judith helped her to her feet. After she was fully erect and had gained her balance, the woman wobbled towards the oven, where the bread and stew were cooking.

The man ordered Judith into the corner where the woman had been sleeping and commanded her to stay there. Frightened, Judith did exactly what she was told, while nervously eying him. He then removed his tie and jacket and dropped them on a chair. Watching him emerge from his western disguise brought to mind stories of girls her age being abducted by men like him. The stories came back vividly, in raw detail, just as frighteningly as they had been told to her.

Bowing her head, Judith held back her tears and began to pray silently. *Dear Lord, help me. Show me the way home. Please, God. I beg you. I promise, if you do, I will never do anything foolish again.*

Locked in a fetal position, her two legs pressed tightly against her chest, Judith glanced furtively around the room. *You mustn't cry,* she kept telling herself. *This isn't the time for tears. This is the time to plan her escape.*

While the two men ate, she looked around the room in search of an exit. It was a small room with only one door that led into the walled courtyard. Even if she made a run for it while the men were eating, she would never be able to get very far without being caught. And even if she were lucky enough to escape, she still had no idea in which direction to head for safety. All she knew was that she was a long way away from Shamash. Without a compass to guide her, she would never be able to find home again.

Her gaze locked on the two men while they ate. They were devouring food voraciously, stuffing themselves as though they hadn't eaten for days. The woman stood at attention near them, a pregnant statue with an empty stare, trained to serve them on request.

When she made eye contact with Judith, her empty eyes unexpectedly opened wide enough to reveal a maternal side.

Could she be the answer? Judith thought, noting her friendliness. *But what could she do? She was pregnant, too subservient to her husband to be of any real help.*

After eating, the ox-cart driver released a noisy belch. He glanced at Judith, huddled in the corner, and smiled at her in a strange, vulgar way, like a wild animal ready to pounce on its prey. "We really got a pretty one this time, Ghulam," he said, scratching his long unkempt beard. "How about letting me break her in?"

"Forget it, Naseer. You aren't getting near her. She's worth too much money unspoiled."

Naseer turned to Ghulam. "How much do you think we'll get?"

"I don't know. I will find out tomorrow when I meet with the buyer."

"Make sure you get plenty. We got ourselves a beauty this time."

"Don't worry about that. You can bet I'll negotiate hard."

Judith broke her silence and interrupted the men unexpectedly. "My daddy's rich," she said. "He'll pay you anything you want for my return."

Ghulam laughed. "That's what they all say, until we talk money. Then it's another matter."

The pregnant woman, who was still observing Judith, didn't notice Ghulam signaling her for more tea. "*Kahba!*" he said, banging on the table with his fist when she didn't respond. "Bring me some tea. I want some *now!*" Startled, she jumped to attention, nearly knocking over the samovar that was next to her. This made her husband angry. "In my glass, not on the floor." She hurried to him, grabbed his glass, and filled it with tea.

After they finished their tea, the woman washed the men's hands, lit their water pipes, and waited nearby for further instructions. Contented, the two men finally rose from the table and went outside to talk privately. The woman then served Judith some of the leftover food, which Judith refused.

"Eat," the woman said. "It's good."

Judith pushed the bowl away from her. "I am not hungry."

"You must eat," the woman said in a motherly voice. "You need your strength."

Judith yielded and took a few mouthfuls of the lamb stew, but she couldn't hold it down. It rose from her stomach almost instantly and emptied back into her bowl.

"I'll get you some tea and rice," the woman said. "That should calm your stomach."

Judith ignored the tea and picked at her rice. Frightened, she asked: "What will they do to me?"

"The pretty ones are usually married off."

"The others?" Judith asked apprehensively.

"The others." She lowered her gaze, ashamed. "The others are sold to brothels."

"I don't want to end up like that," Judith said, crying. "I want to go home to my mamma.."

Sadina placed her hand over Judith's. "You mustn't cry." She pushed away some hair, which fell over Judith's cheek. "You must be brave and accept your fate like me. It's the will of Allah."

"But I am not a Mohammedan. I'm a Christian."

"You must forget your God and become a Mohammedan. You'll be safer then."

"Never!" Judith said firmly. "I will never forsake Him and end up like you."

She felt ashamed for insulting the woman. But Judith couldn't help herself. This was what she feared could happen to her, if she didn't escape.

The woman lowered her gaze in shame. "Perhaps you're right. My lot isn't that good, is it?"

That evening Judith didn't sleep well. She was haunted by nightmares that left her trembling and breathing heavily as though she had been running great distances, chased down dark streets and along lonely roads. The voice of a *muezzin* in the distance was summoning her to prayer. His call was coming from the minaret of a mosque in a nearby village.

"There is no God except Allah," the *Muezzin* was chanting. "Allah is the greatest. Rise up for prayer. Rise up for salvation."

His voice was sonorous and controlled, beckoning her to him in the name of Allah. Each phrase the *Muezzin* chanted began with a limited tonal range and ended with him taking one syllable and lifting it to a brilliant and high finish. She had heard this call for prayer many times, but this was the first time she felt compelled to respond to it and run to it.

Her nightmare abruptly ended when she awoke with a start. Through the skylight, Judith could hear the voice from her dreams chanting the *adhan* in the distance. At first, after the abrupt awakening, she was confused as to where she was. Slowly, Judith began to remember when she surveyed her surroundings in the early dawn and saw the man and woman sleeping next to her. She panicked at the thought of what lay ahead.

If only she could figure out a way to reach the skylight, she might have a chance to escape. Once on the house top she could follow the connecting roofs to the outskirts of the village and then jump to freedom. But if she is successful, and she does make it out of the house, which way should she run? All she knew with any certainty was that Shamash was in the opposite direction from the mountains.

She worried about what could happen to her if she did break free. Her fate then could be more frightening than what she faced now. She mustn't think about that, Judith told herself. She knew that when the opportunity came, she would have to make a run for it. On her own, she might have a chance of reaching home safely. But here, at the mercy of those men, she was doomed.

Judith looked up at the skylight, at what she believed was her window to freedom. *But how would she ever reach the skylight without a ladder – and without being seen?*

The man awoke from his sleep while Judith was pondering her escape. He turned to his wife and shook her. "What is it, Ghulam?" the woman asked, startled.

"Get up!" he commanded. "I want something to eat."

"But it's barely daybreak."

"I must leave early," he said. "I have a long way to travel."

"What about the girl? Will you be taking her?"

"No, she will stay with you. Naseer will be outside, guarding the door."

His wife didn't say anything. She prepared his meal and served it to him silently. While he ate, he looked at Judith several times with a familiar smile, which he held for an uncomfortably long period of time. Embarrassed, Judith hid her body under a blanket of rugs.

"Why do you stare at me like that?" she asked nervously.

"Because you are a very pretty girl, and I would like to enjoy you."

"I won't let you. I'd fight you."

Her attitude of defiance amused him. "With what," he said, "those dainty little hands?" He was a strong man, like the field workers at her father's village. Judith knew she would be helpless against him if ever he decided to take her – no matter how hard she resisted. "Don't worry, my little saint. You have nothing to fear from me. I have a buyer who wants you chaste, and chaste you will be, if I want my bag of gold."

"Why don't you see my daddy? He'll pay you more. He'll double your price, give you anything you want, if you take me to him safely."

"That is very tempting, if true," he said. "But believe me, I will be getting enough from my buyer to satisfy my needs."

"Who is this buyer you want to please? Is he someone I may know?"

"You'll learn in time, so be patient, my pretty one. Now I must go. I have a long journey ahead."

Sadina seemed relieved when her husband left. She turned to Judith. "You can relax," she said. "He will be gone most of the day."

"Where is he going?"

"I don't know. I stay out of his business. It's better that way."

Sadina disappeared into her private thoughts. Her expression grew heavy with sadness, and her eyes filled with tears. Disturbed by the woman's unhappiness, Judith attempted to comfort her. "Please don't cry," Judith said. "I don't like to see you cry."

"I'll be fine. It passes." The woman looked at Judith affectionately. "You are a kind girl. Here, you are about to be sold into slavery, and you worry about me."

"That's because we are alike, you and I. Soon I will be just like you, Sadina – forced to serve someone like Ghulam. I know I will be miserable. It is only natural. Tell me, Sadina. Haven't you ever tried to escape? I know I would try every chance I got."

"There's no point in it. My life wouldn't be any better if I did escape."

"You are wrong, Sadina. Let me prove it to you. Let's get away together while we have a chance. We mustn't allow evil men like Ghulam to control us."

"I can't," she said. "It's not the will of Allah."

"You are wrong. A kind woman like you deserves a better life."

"He's all I've got. Without him, I am alone." Sadina withdrew into her thoughts again. When she returned, she brought more tears with her. "Without him, there is no one."

The woman suddenly began to vomit into a bowl. Judith held Sadina's long hair away from her face. The smell and the sight of her vomit nauseated Judith. She had to fight a rising urge to vomit as well. She looked away and held her nose with two fingers. When the urge passed, Judith prepared some chai for them.

"Drink the chai," Judith said. "It'll help."

The woman merely looked at her affectionately. "You are most kind, Judith. Thank you."

After helping the woman clean herself, Judith sat next to her and they talked.

"What's the name of this village?" Judith asked.

"It's called Al-Shahah."

"I've never heard of it. Where is it, exactly?"

"It's near the Village of Thieves in the Zagros Mountains." Judith became frightened. She had heard about that village. It was where those Christian girls were taken before her father rescued them. Shocking stories of what the Kurds did to the women they captured often circulated in Shamash, and she suddenly had doubts that escaping captivity here would actually lead to freedom.

Regardless, Judith knew that if she valued her life, she would have to try escaping while Ghulam was away. Every minute counted. But how could she ever get away with that foul-looking Naseer guarding the door outside? She looked up at the skylight. That was the only way out, she thought. *But how would she reach it?*

She knew her only hope for escape depended on gaining Sadina's assistance. But would the woman assist willingly? Her husband would turn on her cruelly if Judith escaped. Somehow Judith had to convince the woman to leave with her. But how wise would that be? Sadina couldn't travel far in her condition.

On top of that, the woman would only slow down their travel, endangering them both. Yet Judith had no other moral choice. If she were to escape, she would have to take Sadina with her.

She had no idea where Shamash was or how to get there. Somehow she would have to figure that out. Just thinking about what could happen to her if she didn't escape gave Judith sufficient motivation to want to try. But before she could try, she needed to convince Sadina to join her by assuring her that together they *could* make it to safety.

"Why do you remain here with such a cruel man?" Judith asked pointedly. "Why don't you and I run away together while we still have the chance?"

"Be sensible, Judith," the woman said. "How far can I travel, even if I wanted to leave?"

"You must trust me. Somehow we'll find a way."

"Nonsense. We will never make it. I could deliver at any time."

"We'll worry about that when it happens. We mustn't worry about problems that we don't have yet. You must make a decision, Sadina. This is your opportunity to be free. Do you really want to remain here as Ghulam's servant for the rest of your life?"

"It's the will of Allah."

"Your Allah can't be that cruel to force such a fate on you. Surely He will show you the way, just as my Lord will show me the way. Come, Sadina. Together we will find safety."

"It's impossible!"

"Of course it is," Judith said, "if you allow yourself to believe that. But you mustn't think negatively. You must be strong and willing to take a chance."

"I can't. If Ghulam catches me, he will stone me to death for dishonoring him."

Judith gasped, horrified at the thought of someone crushing Sadina with stones; yet she had no doubt that Ghulam would do it if given a reason. "What about your parents? Won't they protect you?"

"They have no right to protect me. They've sold all their rights to me to Ghulam."

"If you won't think of your safety, what about the safety of your child? Doesn't he deserve a better life than this?"

The woman seemed amazed by Judith's fearlessness. "Who is this God you have who makes you so courageous?"

"He is a kind God, and He will reserve a place for you in His Kingdom, if you accept Him as your savior."

"You believe that?"

"Yes, it says so in the Bible. Those who believe in Him will ascend to heaven in a whirlwind, like Elijah."

"How comforting that must be for you. I've been told that I am nothing more than a soulless dog that will cease to be one day."

"You are wrong. You have a soul, and your soul will live forever. What sort of religion is Mohammedanism if you are taught to believe otherwise?"

"My husband tells me that, and I have no reason to doubt him."

"Well, he lies to you so that he can keep you enslaved. You must cast your lot aside and join me. Let my Lord watch over you. Come with me, Sadina. We'll run away together."

"Impossible! I have nowhere to go. No one to take care of me."

"I will see to it that you are safe in my home. We have a big house with enough room for both you and your child. Let's leave together, Sadina. By the time your husband discovers we are gone, we'll be safely in my house."

Sadina paused and gazed inward. She was obviously struggling with doubt.

"I'll never make it.," Sadina said. "I just don't have the strength."

"I'll be your strength," Judith said confidently. "Just lead me from here, and I'll take you safely to Shamash."

Chapter 13

The Escape

Judith experienced a surge of excitement the moment she broke free from captivity. She was in control once again, and she was able to make her own decisions. What lay ahead was a mystery lined with life-threatening obstacles. Yet, by comparison to what she had left behind, it seemed a hundred times better.

Still, she couldn't relieve herself of a persistent fear, the fear of the unknown, which settled over her once she and Sadina were on the rooftops hurrying to the edge of the village.

Aware of the danger ahead, Judith felt that the added responsibility of having Sadina with her made it necessary for her to be extremely vigilant to any unusual surprises. Judith knew – if she dropped her guard, another Ghulam could appear, and he could be even more dangerous than the two men she and Sadina had left behind. This made it urgent that they travel through the Plain invisibly by avoiding contact with others whenever possible.

Like Sadina, Judith had never left her village alone. The Plain was a mystery, a foreign land of orchards, villages, rivers, and roads. When she and Sadina climbed the ladder to freedom, Judith saw hope beyond the walls of Al-Shahah. With their identities hidden under burkas, the two women resembled all the other Mohammedan women in the Plain. This left them free to travel incognito.

Although Sadina was having trouble keeping up with Judith, she too was caught up in the excitement of breaking free. Once she had made up her mind to leave, Sadina remained resolute and never wavered for a moment by brooding about her fate. Through her actions, she had convinced Judith that she was ready to accept whatever lay ahead. They both agreed that it could only be better than what they had left behind, providing they took no foolish chances.

In the street below, there was some noisy activity. Sadina suddenly stopped to stare at what was unfolding. A woman with a shaven head and a blackened face was sitting on a donkey which was being led through the streets by a man. The crowd was making a high-pitched trilling sound created by the rapid movement of the tongue.

"What's happening, Sadina?" Judith asked.

Sadina stared at the activity below and became visibly upset. "That woman is going to be stoned."

Judith let out a gasp, loud enough to be heard, but not loud enough to rise above the noise below. "That can't be true," Judith said, horrified. "What could she have possibly done to deserve that?"

"Almost anything," Sadina said, immobilized by fear. "It could have been as simple as just disobeying her husband."

Judith grabbed Sadina's hand, which was cold and sweaty. "Come. We must leave before Naseer spots us. I don't want anything horrible like that to happen to you."

Although Sadina hesitated as though she were having second thoughts, she was obviously smart enough to realize that it was too late to turn back. She had freed Judith, and that in itself would be reason enough for severe punishment.

Judith gave a gentle tug to Sadina's hand, and they quickly traveled across the roofs to the village edge.

"We must travel east," Judith said. "Towards Lake Urmia."

"I don't know where that is," Sadina said.

The mountains loomed ahead of them. Judith was reminded of the notorious Village of Thieves once again. Being so close to it sent a chill through her. The last thing she wanted to do was head in the wrong direction. "It's away from the mountains in the same direction the river flows," Judith said. "Does that help?"

"You mean the Shahar River?"

"Yes, of course," Judith said, excited. "The Shahar River. Do you know where it is?"

"The streams irrigating the orchard are fed by that river."

"Wonderful!" Judith said. "That makes it all so simple. All we need to do is follow the streams to the river and the river away from the mountains to my home."

Traveling through the orchards to the river took a while. They walked past large vineyards with neat rows of grape vines and fruit trees, irrigated generously by streams and brooks fed by the river. They passed large fields of wild flowers and wheat stalks, which danced in the wind. It didn't take long before Sadina grew tired. While they followed the stream to the river, she stumbled several times and almost fell. Fortunately, Judith caught her before Sadina could injure herself or her unborn baby.

En route to the river, Judith picked fresh fruit. When they finally reached the river's edge, they both sat on boulders and enjoyed what they had picked. During the respite, they temporarily put aside their worries and amused themselves like two schoolgirls, pausing for refreshments after an invigorating hike.

This schoolgirl moment of pleasure passed unexpectedly when Judith saw a man on horseback ride towards them. *Could that be Naseer?* Judith wondered. *Could he have discovered their disappearance so soon?*

"Someone is coming," Judith said.

"Where?"

Judith pointed in the direction of the mountains.

"Do you think it's Naseer?" Sadina asked.

"I can't tell. He's too far away. If it is Naseer, we'll find out soon enough."

"What shall we do?"

Judith didn't see anywhere nearby to hide. There were only a few small boulders by the water's edge. None were large enough to conceal them. All they could do was stay where they were and remain calm. The man had probably already seen them. If they tried to hide from him, it might only confirm that the two women in burkas were Judith and Sadina. It was important that they appear to be just two Mohammedan women innocently enjoying a little time alone together by the water.

"We mustn't panic," Judith said. "If we do, we will only expose ourselves." A small riverboat was traveling downstream towards them. It was coming very close to where they were standing. "There's a boat," Judith said. "Maybe I can stop it."

"You mustn't," Sadina said. "We could put ourselves in danger."

The horseback rider was coming closer, faster. He had the same unruly beard and hair and wore the same colorful tribal clothes as Naseer. "We have no choice," Judith said, "that man on horseback *is* Naseer."

"You go. I'll stay. It will be better that way."

"Absolutely not. We will travel together and take our chances together. You know what will happen if Naseer catches us. At least, we have some hope with a stranger."

"But it could be dangerous…"

"Would you rather face the possibility of being stoned to death?" Sadina shook her head. Judith waved to the boat captain, calling for his assistance. "I have a pregnant woman here," she shouted. "I must get her to a doctor right away. Can you help us?"

The boat slowed down and headed towards the shore. When Judith looked up, Naseer was only a short distance away. He paused just long enough to evaluate the situation. As the boat lowered its boarding ramp, Naseer began to race towards them.

The minute the boarding ramp hit the shore Judith pushed Sadina towards it, where a man helped her board. "Hurry," Judith said to Sadina. "He's almost here." When Sadina was safely on board, Judith started to run up the ramp.

"Run faster, Judith," Sadina cried out. "Naseer is right behind you."

A hand grabbed Judith by the wrist. When Judith turned, she was glaring into Naseer's angry eyes. "Not so fast, pretty one," he said angrily. "You aren't going to get away that easily."

"Let go of me, you beast," she cried.

"Not on your life," he said.

She plunged her teeth into his hand until she tasted blood. He immediately released her, crying in pain. Enraged, he lunged towards her. At that precise moment, when he was in motion flying towards Judith, a gunshot was heard, and Naseer fell to the water's edge, dead. Without pausing, Judith ran up the ramp into Sadina's arms.

"You are lucky I came along," the boatman said as the boat moved away from the shore. "I've seen that man before. He has a very bad reputation."

Judith was trembling. "He's a terrible man," she said, still in shock. "He was trying to kidnap us."

With Naseer lying on the shore dead, and her and Sadina on a boat with an armed stranger, she wondered what was next. Judith felt no trust for the boatman. After what she had been through, she found it difficult to trust anyone, no matter how honorable they might seem. Her experience in the last two days had heightened her sense of caution with strangers. Although the boatman behaved like a Good Samaritan by coming to their aid, he could still be dangerous, more dangerous than Ghulam and Naseer combined. She couldn't dismiss how quickly and expertly he killed Naseer – *with only one shot.*

"You mustn't worry," he said. "You're both safe now."

"Who are you?" Judith asked suspiciously.

"I'm Behrouz Rahmanian, and I am a rug dealer from Urmia."

"What are you doing so far from the city?"

"I was buying some tribal rugs in the mountains."

"Are you heading back to Urmia?"

"Yes. What about you and your friend? Where are you going?"

"Shamash."

"That's a Christian village."

"Yes, I know. There's a nurse there who will help us."

"Aren't you taking a chance being out alone? It isn't safe for two women to travel so far by themselves."

"You mean there are more men like Naseer on the road?" she asked, acting innocent.

"Absolutely," he said. "I have seen his type before. They are everywhere, looking for stray women."

"You aren't one of those men, are you?" she asked him boldly, observing him to evaluate his reaction.

He smiled; it was a gentle smile without guile. "No, not at all. I am a happily married man with a daughter about your age."

She relaxed and said with relief, "We are most fortunate to have found you."

"Sometimes life surprises you like that, without warning."

Shamash

It was early evening when they reached Shamash. Judith recognized her house in the distance. An enormous sense of excitement came over her – the impossible had happened, she was returning home safely, with a new friend. Once the boat was docked, and she and Sadina were safely on land, she took Sadina's hand and squeezed it. "At last," she said to Sadina. "We have made it to Shamash."

The family had finished dinner, when Judith and Sadina entered the house. Judith didn't realize how hungry she was until she smelled Leah's freshly made stew. During the travel from the village of Al -Shahah to her home, she and Sadina had very little to eat, except for the fresh fruit they had picked in the orchard and some bread the boatman had shared with them.

As she led Sadina through the hall to the parlor, Judith heard her mother scolding Sag. "Bad dog," Abigail said. "Sit! I said sit." She unexpectedly raised her voice. "*Sag, come back here this instant.*"

Sag, who normally responded to family commands, wasn't listening. He could be heard racing through the house into the hall. When he saw Judith, he leaped on her before she could say a word, knocking her to the floor. He then began to lick her face generously with his long wet tongue, as though he were lapping water from a bowl, while wagging his tail vigorously.

Sadina let out a frightened scream, which immediately brought Abigail into the room. Abigail pulled the dog off Judith. "Stop, Sag," she said. "Leave the lady alone."

"Yuck," Judith said, sitting up and wiping her face dry. "His breath is terrible."

"Judith!" her mother exclaimed. "Is that really you?"

Judith removed her head cover. A profound joy, which began deep within her, rose and broke free. "Yes, Mamma. It's me, Judith."

Abigail collapsed onto the floor and brought her daughter close, kissing her and rocking her in her arms as if Judith were still her little baby. All her reserve disappeared as she filled the hall with cries of pleasure. "You are home. My Judith is home at last."

All the strength that Judith had mustered to make it safely home disappeared. She was no longer the courageous young girl who took the initiative to break free of her captors. She was little Judith again, her mother's darling daughter who had just awakened from a nightmare. Secure in her mother's arms, protected again from the world by her mother's infinite strength, Judith let all the pain and fear that she had contained rush out in one overwhelming burst of emotion. "Mamma, I was so scared."

"Of course you were, darling," she said, as she continued to rock her.

"It was terrible, Mamma," Judith said, crying. "*Terrible!* That evil man wanted to enjoy me."

Abigail stopped rocking her daughter and studied her with concern. "He didn't do anything to you? You are all right, aren't you? Tell me, Judith. *You are all right?*"

"I'm , Mamma. Fine."

"Men like that do things which they shouldn't do to young girls. He didn't touch you improperly, did he?"

"No, Mamma. I'm fine. Honest."

Abigail brought her daughter close again, rocking her in her arms. "*Praise the Lord.*"

"Sadina saw to that."

"Sadina?" Her mother pulled away again. "Who is Sadina?"

For the first time, Abigail noticed the woman in the corner, who was completely covered in black. Sadina stepped forwards bashfully.

"That's Sadina, Mamma. That's the nice woman who helped me get away," Judith said tearfully. "I don't know what I would've done if it weren't for her. That man planned horrible things, Mamma, and Sadina saved me from him by helping me escape."

Abigail rose to her feet to greet the woman properly. "How very kind of you," she said.

"Your daughter deserves all the credit," Sadina said. "She is the one who saved both of us."

"Were you also kidnapped by this man?"

"No," Sadina said, embarrassed. "I was married to him."

"It must've been horrible for you."

"It was." She lowered her gaze, embarrassed "This is a man who finds pleasure in doing terrible things to women."

"What kind of things?"

"Terrible things. Too terrible to talk about."

"Do you know who was going to buy my daughter?"

"All I know is that he is someone important, and he is going to pay my husband a great deal of money for her."

"I wish you knew more," Abigail said. "Knowing who it might be could make it easier for us to protect Judith from him."

"Only my husband knows that."

"Maybe my husband should talk to him."

"Mamma, you mustn't, for Sadina's sake," Judith said, rising to her feet. "You'll only let him know where she's hiding."

"You're right," Abigail said to Judith. "We must remain silent. If this man wants you enough, he'll try again. Next time we'll be ready." Abigail turned to the woman. "Thank you for being a friend to my daughter. You are truly an angel." She hugged the woman. *"Welcome to Shamash."*

"You're most kind," Sadina said. "But I fear I'll be a burden. I'm pregnant, and I'll soon be with a child."

"I don't want to hear anything more about the matter. You and your child will be our honored guests as long as you wish to stay here. So dismiss such fears. We will talk about it later at length. Right now you must eat. I am sure you are both starving." Abigail turned to her daughter. "Judith, take her into the kitchen and see to it that Leah prepares something special for both of you. In the meantime, I'm going to share the good news with the family."

For the first time in her adult life, Abigail moved through the house as rapidly as her long skirt permitted her. "She's home," she said when she found Miriam alone, reading the Bible. "She's home, Mother."

"Judith?" Miriam asked.

"Yes, Mother. Your prodigal granddaughter, Judith."

Her mother's face brightened the room like sunshine. "Praise the Lord." She rose quickly from her chair. "Where is she, Abigail? Where is my darling child?"

"First, Mother," Abigail began, "there's something I want to say."

Miriam looked at her daughter, obviously concerned by Abigail's solemn attitude. "What is it, Abigail?"

"Will you ever forgive me for my behavior towards you?"

"Forgive you? For what? For being a loving mother who was worried about her daughter?"

"But I behaved so poorly."

"You behaved as any mother would. You were worried and frightened for the welfare of your daughter. You mustn't apologize for that."

"But I was shameless towards you …"

"It's over, Abigail. I don't want to hear another word about it." Miriam couldn't hold her excitement any longer. "Now tell me, darling, where is she? Where is my adorable Judith?"

"She's in the kitchen with Leah."

The Village of Al-Shahah

It was late evening when the Governor arrived at the Village of Al-Shahah with Ghulam; he was there to inspect his purchase. With him was his henchman, dressed in a red, loose-fitting robe. A long knife was attached to the henchman's belt. When they entered the house, the Governor immediately saw the ladder leading to the skylight.

"They've got away," Ghulam exclaimed, frightened. "They've climbed to the roof and got away!"

"You fool," the Governor said angrily. "How could you be so careless?"

"I never thought she would use the skylight."

"Your problem is you don't think."

"They can't get far. My wife is pregnant, and she fatigues easily." Ghulam glanced at the henchman standing nearby. The henchman's hand was wrapped around his knife handle.

When the Governor nodded, Ghulam instantly turned white. The henchman responded to the signal quickly and grabbed Ghulam's left arm, pulled it behind him and jerked it upward towards his neck. He then severed Ghulam's neck arteries with the knife and released the body, letting it collapse to the floor, bleeding. It happened so fast and was done so expertly that Ghulam didn't have time to react in self-defense. The two men then left the village quietly and disappeared into the night.

The Shamash Home

Judith spent the morning reading a book on the edge of her father's property, by the Shahar River. Sag was resting in the sun next to her, his head on her lap. Occasionally, she would stroke the dog, and without moving his head, Sag would roll up his eyes towards her. Since her return, Sag had remained by her side. He even began eating heartily again, which he didn't do while she was gone, she was told. As a result, Sag was filling out again, turning into that hefty-looking dog he was before her departure. At night, he would sleep near Judith's bed, which her parents had never permitted before the kidnapping. But now, as an added precaution, they believed it would be prudent to use Judith's loyal friend as her twenty-four hour bodyguard. When she awoke in the night after a nightmare, Sag would often come to her and rest his chin on the bed near her head. At such a moment, Judith would smile and pet him affectionately before falling asleep again.

Just as Sag was her comfort during her troubling nights, Judith's books had become her comfort during her waking hours. Reading about the perils of the delightfully naughty schoolgirl, Mademoiselle Josette Dupré, who was forever getting herself into mischief, was Judith's way of lightening the day.

Despite the temporary pleasure she derived from reading about Josette's charming girlish activities, Judith was still unable to forget her own harrowing experience. A word or thought in the story would trigger a recollection. And the memory would grow like an infection and remind her once again of the danger that lurked outside the village. Life had taken a sharp turn for Judith. The kidnapping had stolen her innocence. By trying to lose herself in the adventures of Josette, Judith was trying to recover her innocence. Although she still found some humor in the story, it wasn't sufficient to satisfy her. The once charming character was becoming a foolish and boring figment of the author's imagination. Seeing Josette plunge herself into situations that could only become regrettable didn't always amuse Judith.

While Judith sat by the river's edge, reading about Josette's foolishness, Sag lifted his head and let out a deep growl, exposing a row of healthy white teeth. Judith looked at the dog curiously, then turned, startled, towards an unexpected sound behind her. She immediately relaxed when she saw who it was.

"Hello, Judith," the Governor said. "How happy I am to learn of your safe return."

"Then you know what happened?"

"Yes, your father told me everything." Sag stood by Judith, alert. The Governor observed the dog nervously. It was obvious he found Sag's low-key growling menacing. "I came the minute I heard you had arrived home safely. How fortunate you are to have escaped."

"I must thank Sadina for that."

"Sadina? Who is Sadina?"

"She's the wife of my kidnapper."

Unexpectedly, he became silent – and uncomfortable. Judith wondered why. "She helped you?" he asked nervously. Judith nodded, observing him. He tried to conceal his discomfort with a smile, but it was too late. Judith had already made note of it. "How lucky you are to have found such a friend," he added brightly.

"Yes, I agree," Judith said. "My mother thinks so too, and that's why she has invited her to live with us."

She noticed that he suddenly turned pale. His blue, seductive eyes lost their glow. "She's here?"

"Yes, she is sleeping. She tires so easily and must rest a lot."

"Did she say anything about her husband? Why he kidnapped you?"

"Nothing, except that someone wanted to buy me."

He was relieved. "You weren't harmed?" he asked anxiously. "You are all right, aren't you?"

"Yes, I'm all right." She noticed Sag was still eying the Governor menacingly.

"I'm so glad to hear that," he said, pleased.

She frowned. "But I still find it hard to forget."

"You must forget. It's in the past. You are safe now." His face lit up with the handsome charm she had always remembered. "Let me help you forget. How would you like to enjoy a special welcome-home surprise?"

She paused and looked at him curiously. She remembered the last time someone had a surprise for her. "What kind of surprise?" she asked cautiously.

He looked at the house, then at Sag. "I bought a new riverboat. I would love to take you for a ride.

Would you like that? Just the two of us. It will be such fun."

"A new boat," she said. "I love boats." Her curiosity was piqued. "Where is it?"

"It's right over there, at the pier, next to your father's boat. Would you like to see it?" Sag began to growl when the Governor extended his hand to help Judith to her feet.

Judith held back her hand, and rose by herself. She remembered the scene at the Bible Doll Shop when Ghulam took her hand and wouldn't let go. Even though this was different, and this was the Sardar and a friend of the family, she still hesitated at accepting his gracious gesture. Something about the Governor disturbed Sag. Judith had no idea what it was. Until she knew, she decided to heed Sag's warnings and remain alert.

"I would love to see your boat, but at another time," she said politely. "I need to return to the house. I've been gone most of the morning and my mother will worry if I don't return soon." His gentle smile hardened, revealing a hint of desperation, which made her uncomfortable.

"It need only be for a minute," he said, trying to conceal his desperation with a warm smile. "Come, let me show it to you." He reached out again to take her hand. His sudden movement startled Judith, and she stepped back. Sag growled dangerously.

"Another time," she said, backing away from him in the direction of the house.

He moved forward towards her, still smiling, still observing her with his unsettling look. "Why are you so afraid? Don't you trust me?"

"I am not afraid," Judith said bravely.

"You are shivering."

"It's getting cold outside."

"Here, put on my jacket," he said, removing it. A gun was strapped to his waist. She stared at it, surprised. He looked down at it and smiled. "Sometimes I must carry it, when I travel around the Plain. I never know who may want to rob me."

She was suspicious. The only time she had ever seen her father with a gun was when he was hunting. Why would the Governor have one? He didn't need to travel with a gun. He had bodyguards to protect him.

He quickly changed the subject. "Come, let's go for a boat ride together. We'll have a wonderful time. I promise."

Judith continued to back away from him. "I told you I can't. My mother is expecting me."

"If you come," the Governor said with a smile as handsome as he was insistent, "I will delight you with a thousand and one stories that will be more enjoyable than anything you could ever read in your books."

Judith was intrigued. It would be such a pleasant way to forget the past, drifting on the water while listening to him tell stories. But once again she hesitated. She removed the governor's jacket and returned it to him. "I can't," she said. "I must get home."

"Is this how you treat the Governor – by rejecting his kind offer?"

"My mother would disapprove."

"I will send my servant to her and tell her where we are going so that she won't worry."

His compelling blue eyes, his handsome Grecian features made him more attractive than any man Judith had ever seen. Yet she was frightened by him. Why?

"I said I can't," she said firmly. Judith was about to run to the house, when he grabbed her hand and pulled her to him.

She dropped her book. "Let go of me," she cried, kicking and swinging with her free arm.

At the precise moment when he was bringing her close, Sag leaped on him, and the Governor released her to defend himself against the dog. Judith immediately ran towards the house. A few moments later, she heard a shot. When she turned to see what had happened, she saw that the Governor was bleeding at the neck, and Sag was lying on the ground.

"Sag!" she cried out hysterically. "Come to me, Sag. Please come to me." But Sag didn't move. The Governor quickly disappeared as the servants ran out of the house.

Chapter 14

The American Mission, Urmia, Winter

General Field Marshall Boris Yedemsky was worried. He knew what would follow when he heard the announcement. His many years in the military taught him to be alert to all signs leading to open war. A month after joining forces with the Central Powers, Sultan Mehmed V, brother to the dethroned Sultan Abdul Ahmid, puppet leader of the Young Turks, spiritual leader of Islam, chosen successor of Mohammed, announced to the world a *jihad* against the non-Muslim enemies of Islam – namely, the British, the French, and the Russians. His proclamation was delivered publicly as a *fatwa* by Sheikh al-Islam, and it was posted on government buildings everywhere, including the Plain.

When Boris Yedemsky read the *fatwa*, he knew a holy war would soon follow. There wouldn't be a Muslim anywhere who wouldn't answer yes to the questions in the *fatwa*.

"If Muslims live in a country that is an enemy of Islam," the proclamation read, "should they not rise up and take arms against this country? If Muslims are massacred or captured by the enemies of Islam, should they not all unite and kill these enemies? And if Muslims refuse to fight, should they not be subject to the anger of Allah and to His divine wrath?"

As a result of this *fatwa*, large groups of Christians left Turkey for Persia. When the General Field Marshal interrogated them at the border, they all told him the same horrible stories. These stories were repeated to him in detail, not by one or two lonely voices, but instead by a chorus of men and women and children who made it over the Zagros Mountains to safety in the Plain. In his many years in the military, he had never heard such stories of brutality against any group. They spoke of rivers overflowing with the swollen bodies of babies, of wells being stuffed with human remains, and of refugees being stripped and deported to the south and abandoned in the desert, where they were left to die of hunger and thirst. All in the name of Allah, and on a scale greater than anything even the Crimson Sultan would have considered doing against the Armenians in the 1890s.

At the American Mission in Urmia, Boris Yedemsky shared these stories with the Reverend Michael Johnson. It was obvious to the General that the Reverend wasn't comfortable with the subject, and that he was worrying about all the Christians still in Turkey, some of whom were missionaries and friends.

"I too worry," Boris Yedemsky said with painful solemnity. "Everything I hear confirms that Constantinople is determined to massacre every last Christian." He gazed into the frightened eyes of the

Reverend, and he was saddened by the news he would have to relate. "None of this looks good," the General Field Marshal continued. "From what Moscow tells me, a land attack by the Turks is imminent, and it could be as destructive as their naval attack was in the Black Sea."

The Reverend nervously wrung his hands together as though they were cold. "Does Moscow have any idea where this attack will occur?"

"We think it will be nearby."

The Reverend turned white with fear. "The Plain?"

"No, not the Plain. In the north, probably in the Caucasus."

"The Armenians?"

"That's what we believe."

"Those unfortunate souls, how they suffer for their faith!"

"You are right, Reverend. The Turks have shown no kindness towards them."

"Do you think it will ever change?"

"*Nyet!*" Boris said firmly. "Their hatred has been too ingrained. It has been nurtured over too many centuries to change."

"Then you see no hope for peace?"

"None."

"What will become of us?"

"I have no idea. All I know with some degree of certainty is that if my report is accurate, I may have to relocate my troops to the Caucasus." Boris paused, disturbed by what he was about to say. "This could endanger the life of every Christian remaining here."

"We'll be slaughtered," Michael said, frantic with fear. "The Turks and the Kurds will descend from the mountains and butcher every last one of us."

"Yes," Boris said, nodding sadly. "It could become bloody."

The General was a man who had fought many battles and had received The Order of St George from Tsar Nicholas II for his valor. Instead of being hardened by all the suffering he had seen, he merely became more sensitive to the plight of war victims. Tears came to his eyes when he spoke to the Reverend. The General knew how vulnerable the Christians were without Russian protection. "You mustn't worry yet, Reverend. Nothing is settled," he said in a comforting tone. "This might all pass. I tell you this not to frighten you, but to prepare you in case it occurs. I suggest you discuss this matter with your elders. But be assured of one thing. If I should ever leave, I will leave you our entire arsenal."

"What good is an arsenal to us? We are men of God. We have no fighting skills."

"Then you must hide somewhere."

"But where? There's no safe place anywhere for us."

"Why not stay here? The Turks would never be so foolish as to provoke the Americans by attacking their mission."

"But there are so many of us and so little space. What will happen to those who can't make it here?"

Boris Yedemsky knew what would happen. The powerful forces of the Turks would sweep down on them and wipe them out. Such was the nature of war. Such was the nature of the Islamic army.

"I have no answer for you, Reverend," he said in a heavy voice. "All I can offer for comfort is that, when I get my orders to leave, I will notify you immediately."

La Sublime Porte, Constantinople

The Minister of Interior observed Gazi Demir with dark, alert eyes that peeked from beneath his untamed black eyebrows. Kudret Kaya was a huge man who looked obese next to the trim muscularity of Gazi. "Your plan didn't work," Kudret said. "The Muslims in the colonies didn't turn against their European rulers. Even the Emir of Mecca denounced the *jihad*, claiming it was absurd to wage a holy war against Christians with a Christian country like Germany on your side. Your scheme for a world-wide jihad failed. Now what will you do?"

"I will proceed as planned," Gazi said, unruffled by the Minister's reminder. "Next month I will lead an attack against the Russians myself in the Caucasus."

"That's insane," Kudret said, stunned. "The snow and freezing temperatures will make fighting in the mountains impossible."

Gazi sat perfectly erect, his hands folded neatly on his lap – a war leader who seemed absolutely convinced of the sensibility of his decision. "It will be a challenge. But a challenge I must accept to gain a military advantage in the Caucasus. The Russians won't expect anyone to attack during the winter, and they will be totally unprepared." He smiled confidently. "It should be an easy victory."

Kudret leaned forward slowly to reach for his glass of tea. His chair wasn't sturdy enough to handle the stress brought about by the shifting weight of his large and powerful body and it began to wobble a little. "How does the Kaiser feel about your plans?"

"He doesn't know."

"You didn't tell him? Aren't you worried he will be furious when he learns? You will be acting without his orders, expanding your reach beyond our borders for your own personal gain. Such a breach of trust will infuriate him."

"On the contrary," the Pasha said. "He will love it, because it will draw Russia's attention away from the Polish and Galician fronts. This will give the Germans an enormous advantage in Europe, which will please him."

The chair creaked as Kudret leaned back, sipping his tea. He thoughtfully weighed what Gazi had said. "How can you be sure of that? The Kaiser is unpredictable. You never know how he will react to anything."

"I agree!" Gazi said. "That's why I took the liberty of bestowing on him the title Hajji Wilhelm, the benevolent protector of Islam."

Kudret looked at him, puzzled. "What does that have to do with the matter?"

"It's very simple, my friend. He loves his titles. Wearing a fez and playing caliph should keep him entertained while I plan my attack," Gazi said. "When he does discover what I have done, the battle will be over, and I will remind him only of the results. That's all that will matter at that point."

Kudret noted how it pleased Gazi, a gatekeeper's son, to be in a position to outsmart the powerful Prussian Hohenzollern.

"In many ways," Gazi added, "the Kaiser is really only a vain schoolboy with a loud bark."

"Yes, but with a deadly bite."

"Believe me, Kudret, his anger will pass after I have successfully defeated the Russians in the Caucasus, and after the Germans gain their advantage on the Polish and Galician fronts."

"Surely you aren't so foolish to believe that a victory in the Caucasus will be that easy. Even a surprise attack against the Russians won't guarantee you success. The area is mountainous, and the Russians have a strong military presence there. Aren't you concerned about the possibility of defeat?"

"Be assured, I will defeat them," Gazi said. "I will use the Prussian and Napoleonic tactics I learned from the Germans, and I will encircle their stronghold in Sarikami and attack from three or more different positions all at once."

"But what about the weather? It's freezing there in the winter. Your troops will die from exposure to the cold."

"There will be losses, it's true, but with Prussian training and supplies, we should be fine."

Kudret set his cup and saucer on the table. "You are taking an enormous chance for such an insignificant battle."

"This won't be an insignificant battle. It will be the turning point of the war for us. By launching a decisive attack in the Caucasus, I will force the Russians guarding the Plain to relocate to the North to fight in the battle. This will leave the Plain wide open for my other regiment to take." He smiled. "With the assistance of my Muslim allies in the region, *it will be a slaughter!*"

"Have you ever given any thought to the possibility of failure?"

"I never think about failure," Gazi said. "I only think about success and the future of the Ottoman Empire."

The Zagros Mountains

Together Ejder and his horse were one, a sleek black beast in motion; they traveled from village to village at lightning speed like an unstoppable, evil force from hell. Ejder's cape flew behind him in the wind as he rode through the snowy, rocky pass, leaping over boulders and frozen creeks, and frightening away wild animals on his path.

Before he even arrived at his destination, the news of his coming had reached the villages on both sides of the mountainous Persian and Turkish border. Most of the villagers were waiting for Ejder, eager to hear what he had to say, and they rushed to greet him the minute they saw him arrive in their village.

He immediately brought his horse to a complete halt. It rose on its powerful hind legs and dropped to all four in one spot, dead still. Surrounded by a worshipping crowd, Ejder enjoyed his moment of glory. Like the *imams* and *softas* who spread the word during their Friday prayers, he too was igniting the minds of the crowd with flaming words of hate. Ejder looked down from his throne atop his horse and released his most deadly weapon of war – *the big lie.*

"What great news does the all-knowing Ejder bring to us today?" one of the warlords asked.

"I'm here to share with you what my friends in high places have shared with me."

"Tell us, Ejder. We are eager to hear your wise words. Speak, my friend. We all want to hear what you have to say."

"I've come to warn you," Ejder said. *"Beware of the Christians in the Plain.* They are using the war in Europe to unite against us."

"How can that be? They are unarmed."

"That is not true. The Russians have been arming them and teaching them how to turn every last Muslim man and boy they capture into eunuchs for their service."

The crowd gasped in horror. "The swine!" they roared.

One villager stepped out of the crowd, which surrounded Ejder, and approached him. "I have heard, O Great One," he said, looking up into the mighty man's eyes, "that they are also violating our young girls by using them for their pleasure in foul and unorthodox ways?"

"It is worse than that," Ejder said to him. "I have just learned from a reliable authority that they are using the blood of these innocent girls to *flavor* their stew."

"Surely you are wrong," the villager said. "Allah would never permit such savagery."

"They spit in His face," Ejder said.

"*They wouldn't dare!*"

"But you are wrong, my friend. *They do dare.* They are even telling everyone that Mohammed is an imposter, not a prophet – an evil force of nature that must be purged from the mind of every last Muslim."

The crowd gasped in horror. "*Such blasphemy!*"

"So you see, my friends, they leave us no choice. We must unite against them and destroy every last one of them," Ejder said. "We can't allow them to pollute the earth with their hatred. It's Allah's wish that we do so. Those of you who join me as Holy Warriors against the infidels will be rewarded in heaven with riches and pleasures beyond anything you have ever dreamed."

Angry fists flew up into the air. "Death to the infidels!" the crowd shouted.

"Death without mercy," Ejder said. He then removed his sword and circled the air with it. *"Jihad!"* he cried out. *"Allāhu Akbar."*

"Jihad!" the crowd screamed back hysterically. *"Allāhu Akbar."*

The Shamash Home, January 1915

Malko no longer had to persuade Abigail that it was time to leave the Plain. After Judith's return, she had changed her mind about remaining in Persia.

"We should leave as soon as possible," Abigail said to Malko. "We can't give the Governor another opportunity to make contact with Judith."

"You're absolutely right, Abigail," Malko said, pleased with her long-awaited decision. "We must leave before the Russians depart."

"Do we still have enough time to get safely to America? It isn't too late, is it, Malko?"

"No one knows for sure how much time we have. Not even the Russians," he said. "That's why we mustn't hesitate. Every minute counts. I will plan the journey. You must sell whatever you can. We will need gold, lots of it."

Malko withdrew to his library to map their escape. Surrounded by books and periodicals, he had everything he needed to begin his research. He started by reviewing in detail maps of Asia and Europe and by reading current newspaper reports of the war activities. Armed with this information, he was in a position to plot an escape. He quickly eliminated the northern route.

Russia was facing huge social unrest, which the war with Germany only briefly quieted. Not known for his strong leadership, Tsar Nicholas seldom responded sensibly to internal problems. Sometimes he lost his focus by indiscriminately killing dissenters. This left many of his people angry. Any moment his subjects could turn against him and revolt. It wouldn't surprise Malko if the rumors he had heard were true and Germany was inciting a revolution in Russia. No, the north would not be a good exit point. The same was true of the Asia-to-the-Pacific route. Traveling through so many countries would take considerable time and create for them enormous obstacles.

The best solution, he believed, was to travel south, follow the pathway of the British to the Persian Gulf and then pass through the Suez Canal into the Mediterranean Sea. To reach the British, they needed to form an armed caravan to protect themselves against petty robbers. There was only one major problem they faced by following the British pathway to freedom – how would they survive the sea voyage? According to news reports, German submarines were becoming a serious problem on the Atlantic. They were sinking foreign ships indiscriminately.

There was no question about it. Regardless of which route they took, they still faced danger. The only route that seemed best, based on current reports, was the southern route. As long as Germany's attention was concentrated on the north, there was a good chance that the family could slip past those submarines in the Atlantic and make it safely to America.

Malko's gaze traveled about the room, noting the books and antiquities, which were so much a part of his life. He wondered what he should take. Important decisions had to be made, quickly. Any moment his circumstances could change. He paused when his attention settled on the painting of the three apostles, and he experienced a deep sadness. The world those apostles had once offered the Assyrians was now disappearing. It was being violated by a new world order. Would Persia survive? Would Europe survive?

"Have you made your decision?" Malko later asked his father-in-law. "Will you and Miriam join us when we leave?"

Daniel removed his pince-nez and placed it on the desk over some notes he was preparing for his next sermon. "I don't think so, my son. It's too late for us. Miriam and I are both too old to run. We will stay here and help Reverend Johnson at the mission – but you and your family must leave. You must take them all to safety."

"Your decision to remain grieves me," Malko said. "It will be a thorny path for us without you and Miriam by our side." Malko looked fondly at the scholarly gentleman who had become like a father to him after his parents' untimely death. To Malko he was a man of infinite wisdom, a religious fountainhead that gave direction and strength to his existence. "Is there nothing I can say or do to persuade you to change your mind?"

"Nothing, my son. But be assured, we will all meet again," Daniel said. "If not in this life, then in the next."

Abigail burst into the room. She was out of breath. "It's happened," she cried out.

"What's happened?" Malko asked with alarm.

"The Russians are leaving."

Journey to Russia

One woman paused before beginning her journey north with the Russians. She looked back beyond the orchards at the walled village she had known most of her life. Tears began to flow and freeze on her cheeks almost instantly.

Her husband put his arm around her. "We'll be fine, Lilith," Haron said, comforting her. "Life will be much easier for us in Russia without the Turks to worry us."

"But everything we have has been left behind," she said tearfully. "Everything we worked so hard to build we must abandon. Why is this happening to us, Haron? What have we done to be punished so severely?" She buried her face in her husband's arms and hung tightly onto him, squeezing from him whatever strength she could.

A child tugged at her coat. "Mamma, I wanna go home," the young girl said, bundled to almost twice her size in clothes. "I'm cold."

The woman stooped to address her daughter face-to-face. "Be brave, Abella," she said. "You must be brave." She fussed with the child's scarf to be sure it covered enough of her face from the harsh wind. "It is time for us to move on."

"But I don't wanna. It's cold, and I wanna go home."

"I know you do, but we must leave."

"But why?"

"It's God's wish."

Lilith lifted Abella into her arms. With her child cuddled close to her, she began what she knew would be a long, hard journey north by foot. She walked alongside her husband, who pulled a two-wheeled cart containing a few of their most needed things.

Ahead of the woman was a long, ragged line of refugees, a huge procession of men, children and women who headed north against a brutally cold wind. They carried with them only what they or their horse-driven sleighs, buffalo wagons or donkeys could hold. All their other possessions were left behind in their villages, as they followed the Russian soldiers towards an uncertain future.

Without an afternoon sun to warm it, the cloudy day grew colder. A merciless northwest wind blasted Lilith with flakes of snow, which froze on her exposed flesh and stuck to her clothes, turning her into a snow woman trekking in slow motion. Lilith knew she had to stay in step with her husband and remain close to the others; otherwise she and her child could disappear into the white blur. It didn't take long for her to realize that carrying her daughter was becoming a serious burden which she was no longer able to tolerate. Lilith was ready to put the child down to give her arms and back a rest, when she realized her daughter was stiff and silent. One of the child's arms clung to her neck. When she moved it, Lilith saw that her little girl was curled up in the same position in which she had been held. Her daughter had turned into a frozen body of ice, a lifeless reproduction of what she had once been.

"She's dead!" Lilith cried out, collapsing into the snow, cuddling her daughter in her arms. "My Abella is dead."

Lilith was rocking the frozen girl in her arms, hoping for some miracle to occur, for her to thaw and come alive. "She's dead," she said to her husband. "Our Abella is dead."

Haron dropped beside her and brought the two of them close to him, weeping quietly. The others moved past the grieving couple, obviously too blinded by the snow and their own sorrow to notice them.

"We mustn't grieve, Lilith," her husband said. "It's best this way. Our Abella is safely home now."

They dug a hole in the soft snow and placed Abella in it. Using several broken limbs from a tree, they made a cross beside the burial site. After saying a short prayer, they returned to their cart and continued their journey northward.

The children and the old were the first to collapse, exhausted and cold. They would just drop to the ground like fallen white statues. Occasionally, a soldier would save a child by lifting him onto his horse and wrapping him in his coat. Many of the others, especially the elderly, would stagger to a tree to rest in the snow, where they would freeze to death, mouth open, eyes staring.

Seeing them freezing to death caused her to cry with grief for them and her daughter, while the others sang sorrowfully:

My heart is aching, I see the storm;
All around me, the ocean roars.
Give me strength, my Lord, to make it home;
For all around me, I see the storm.

The Shamash Home

Judith ran outside where she could be alone, away from the family and all the conversation. Listening to war talk upset her. Her teenage mind needed relief; it needed to forget, even if only temporarily, what was happening around her.

She threw herself into the snow and tried to pretend everything was fine again. Lying on her back staring up at the grey sky, gazing into infinity, Judith felt small, a snowflake in a vast universe. She began to move her arms in the snow to make fan-shaped wings. She wanted to become an angel and fly – soar to heaven – where she could be reunited with Sag.

Light snow was falling, and she caught them in her mouth – small flakes of snow that tasted like cold splashes of water when they melted on her tongue. Suddenly she paused.

Tears came to her eyes. She remembered Sag, how he used to stand close to her and lick the snowflakes from her face. Judith looked around, as though any moment she expected him to hurry towards her and lick her with his huge tongue. But there was no Sag. Their many years together as companions had come to an end. He was gone, her long-time love was dead, shot by that evil governor, and she was alone now. Judith rolled over on her side, curled up into a ball, and cried.

Gunshots interrupted her mourning unexpectedly. They were heard outside the high-wall surrounding the house, and, a few minutes later, from the roof of her house. Judith rose from the ground and stared up at the roof in bewilderment.

Her mother came to the door. Abigail's tone was urgent, her words uncompromising. "Judith, come inside. Now, Judith, *right away.*"

Chapter 15

The Village of Shamash

Abigail was packing frantically. No sooner did she place a dress neatly into her trunk than she yanked it out and tossed it on the bed. Not warm enough. Not practical enough. Think, Abigail. Easy-to-manage clothes. Warm clothes. It's winter.

Several times she burst into tears in frustration. *What colors should I select? How much clothing should I take? Do I have enough room in my trunk for everything? Be practical, Abigail. Practical!*

Sometimes she would just stop packing and lean against the trunk and cry. *It's your fault,* she would tell herself. *No one else's. You brought this on yourself, Abigail Tamras Shamash, by refusing to face the facts. Why? Why did you do this and endanger the safety of the entire family? This could've all been avoided, if you hadn't been so stubborn. All you needed to do was just pack your things and leave when Malko first brought up the subject. But no, no, you had to resist, use all your female wiles to get your way. For what? For this moment?*

During one of these sudden emotional outbursts, while reaching for a handkerchief, she saw Malko standing at the door and silently observing her. She didn't know how long he had been there, but she could see, when their gazes met, that he too was deeply troubled. This startled her. Normally he was confident and in control during crises, a leader, someone to follow during an emergency; today that wasn't the case. He seemed frightened and concerned, unsure of his next move. He handed her a small handgun.

"What's this for?" she asked, puzzled.

"To protect yourself."

"Please, Malko. I don't want it." She dropped the gun on the bed without giving it any further consideration.

"Take it, Abigail. You may need it."

"I wouldn't know what to do with it."

"It's simple. You just aim and pull the trigger."

"I still don't want it."

"Keep it. It'll be your protection until I am with you again."

"When will that be?"

"I don't know. A few days, perhaps. After the Russians and the villagers have enough time to get away."

"You could be killed," she said, frightened.

"I'll be fine."

"Come with us, Malko. *Please*, you'll be safer."

"I can't. This isn't a question of my safety. It's your safety – everyone else's safety. I must remain, Abigail, and slow down the attack."

He stood before her, looking so vulnerable, so sweet, as though he were painfully aware that staying was the worse decision for him to make; all the love he had ever felt for her during their fifteen years of marriage surfaced and released itself in that look. Was this going to be their goodbye? She stroked his curly black hair, felt its luxurious softness against her fingers.

"I won't be able to bear it without you," she said.

"You must be strong, Abigail, for the family's sake. You may have to go on without me one day."

"Don't say that, Malko," she panicked. "Life will be impossible without you."

"Nonsense! You will survive, because you must. So listen carefully. I've something important to share with you," he said. "To make sure you never lack anything, I have buried some gold. It's near the stables, next to the boulder by the apricot tree. There is enough there for you to start a new life."

"Why are you telling me this, Malko? Why are you putting me through this torture?" she said. "I told you. I won't leave without you."

"When the time is right, you will," he said with confidence. "I have contacted my brother, and he is expecting you."

"It's no use, Malko. I won't leave the Plain without you," she said stubbornly. "It's difficult enough going to the mission alone. To say goodbye, perhaps forever, would be torture. As long you remain here, I will remain too. That's final. There's nothing more to say on the subject. *Nothing!*"

"You're being foolishly emotional now," he said. "You'll think differently when it's safe for you to leave. At that time, if I can't lead you, I want you to head south, where the British are, and take the passage across the Zagros from Hamadan to Baghdad and then follow the Tigris to the Gulf. I will meet you in America at my brother's home. Now go. Quickly. You haven't much time."

She was trembling, frightened. She couldn't think clearly. Her entire world was in turmoil. Everything she knew and loved was crumbling. How could she ever continue without him? Malko was her anchor in the storm, her captain during uncertain times. Whenever she needed him, he was always there, ready to spring to life and come to her aid. She couldn't let go of him, even briefly.

"Will you ever forgive me?" she said tearfully.

"Forgive you?" he asked, surprised.

"For not always telling you how much I love you."

"It wasn't necessary, Abigail. I always knew."

"About Dakan as well?"

"About Dakan as well."

"Never have doubts, Malko," she said, stroking his bearded cheek. "It's you I married. It's you I have loved since. No one else. Not even for a moment. Dakan has only been an irritating and often-distant memory."

"You have confirmed that many times and in many wonderful ways."

She smiled gently. "You are a good man, Malko Shamash."

"And you, my dear Abigail Shamash, are a good woman." He pulled away from her, stepped back to gain emotional control of the situation. "Now finish your packing and go. I don't want to hear another word from you."

The troika sleigh, harnessed to three white horses, was ready to leave. Abigail placed the pistol under the fur cover on her lap. Packed tightly in the sleigh with Abigail were Judith, Suzy, Miriam, and Sadina, who was nursing her newborn child. In the other sleighs were the remaining female members of the Shamash household, including relatives.

The sleighs traveled over frozen ravines and brooks with speed and ease. The Valdai bells, attached to the center horse's collar, played a melodic tune. Each one of the bells sounded a little different, but together they created a sonorous symphony in time with the even and quick movements of the horses. Sometimes the sleigh would unexpectedly hit a rock, causing it to bounce and lift everyone from their seats – but without once muddling the symphony of the bells.

While her daughter nestled closely, resting her head on her Persian lamb coat, Abigail remained keenly alert to everything she saw and heard. In the distance, she saw a caravan slowly following the Russians northward to safety and freedom. Like the Shamash family, the members of the caravan were on the run, leaving behind all their earthly possessions for others to claim. The evil forces out to dominate them were rapidly closing in on them to claim power. Without the Russians to protect them, the Christians were doomed.

What she was seeing wasn't new. History books were filled with stories of the mass exoduses of people seeking safety in new lands. For her, it was all déjà vu. Each time, it was the same theme – freedom versus domination, one group against the other. Would it ever end? She could only hope and pray that it would, and that God would show them a little mercy.

The Valdai bells grew softer as the sleigh reduced its speed. A throng of people was collecting at the gate and pushing its way into the walled city of Urmia. Frightened by the confusion, Abigail took hold of the gun resting on her lap under the fur cover and held onto it tightly.

Abigail breathed with ease and released her hold on the gun only after she and the others entered the American Mission compound without incidents. In the wind, flying high above the mission wall, was an American flag, a reminder to the enemy that this was an American mission; any disturbance to it or its inhabitants could provoke the Americans to declare war. This simple but effective statement, conveyed clearly by a red-white-and-blue flag, was seen by Abigail as a heavenly shield that protected them from assault. It amazed her that a piece of cloth could so easily humble their foe. Such was the power of might, she thought.

Beyond the gatekeeper's house was the beautiful wide avenue that led to the main buildings of the mission; it was lined with huge hundred-year-old oriental plane trees. Abigail remembered spending many hot summer days in the shade of the trees, picnicking among the flowers in bloom. As the sleigh slowly moved along the grand avenue, sliding effortlessly over the snow to the rectory, this image of the past was marred by all the refugees swarming the grounds, seeking shelter.

The Reverend Michael Johnson was standing on the rectory porch. Staring at the mass confusion around him, he was deeply agitated when the sleighs arrived. "Abigail, thank the Lord you've come," he said joyfully when her sleigh stopped in front of the rectory. "I've been beside myself, wondering how my mission staff and I would ever take care of all these people."

"Don't worry, Reverend," Abigail said, finding strength in his need. "My family and my staff are here with me. Somehow we'll get through this together."

The Reverend looked relieved. "Bless you, Abigail. Bless you."

The Shamash Village

Before Abigail and the others could seek refuge at the mission, small groups of looters descended on Shamash, eager to take advantage of the Russians' unexpected departure. To their surprise, they were quickly defeated by Malko's well-armed men. Despite this small victory, Malko knew they would return again at the first sign of weakness.

As Malko and his men lay waiting, prepared for another battle, he didn't worry about this small band of opportunistic looters, for they were nothing against his well-armed men; it was the army in the west that was slowly closing in on Shamash that worried him. Would he be able to delay their advance long enough for the others to find safety at the mission or in Russia? Shamash was the last wall of resistance. There was nothing beyond his village to stop the enemy. Once Shamash was defeated, the entire Plain would be theirs to claim.

Camouflaged by the snow blanketing the village, Malko and the villagers waited on the rooftops of their homes for the army to come. While lying on the cold, snow-covered roof in wait, he suddenly realized how lonely it was without the cheerful and friendly sounds of his family. The only sound that broke the silence and interrupted his thoughts was the whistling wind that blew freezing air across the Plain, punctuated intermittently by the pitiful cries of wild animals calling to their mates somewhere in the distance.

Occasionally, small groups of refuges staggered towards the village in search of shelter; they came in twos and fours, sometimes in sixes or eights from western villages, which had been attacked and destroyed by the advancing army. Along the way, they left a brief trail which the drifting snow quickly covered.

By the time they reached Shamash, the new arrivals were exhausted physically and emotionally. They brought with them heartbreaking stories of murder. Although Malko had heard similar reports from Christians before, none seemed quite so horrific as those he was hearing now, because they were reports of what was happening, not in Turkey, but in the Plain.

"Who were these murderers?" Malko asked.

"A mix of Kurds and Turks," one woman said. "They arrived peacefully as friends with their white-crescent-and-star red flag."

"You trusted them?"

"Yes, foolishly. We fell for their sweet words and promises. Unfortunately, we didn't realize that everything they said was a lie, until it was too late. All they really wanted were our guns."

"Did you give them up?"

She lowered her head and covered her face in shame. "We were so stupid." She looked up at Malko and said in defense, "They were so nice and they kept reassuring us that we had nothing to fear."

"What did they do after they got your guns?"

"Nothing immediately. But several days later they returned with a full army. Thousands of them. And they swarmed us from all directions until our village filled with them, and we could no longer see the snow on the ground because of their number." She paused, her voice cracking. "A few of us were lucky. We were able to get away by way of the river."

When they finished telling their stories and recovered some of their strength, Malko armed those who chose to stay and fight, and he gave the others who wanted to leave food and warm clothing for their journey. It tore his heart to see hard-working people driven from their homes by criminals and reduced to such helpless desperation.

The Great War in Europe had finally reached Shamash. Everything he had lived for, everything his ancestors had built, was collapsing in ruin before him. It amazed him that the Assyrians had survived for so long. At some point in time, he would have thought the generational connection to their Christian roots would have been severed by continuous strife with such a savage and lawless enemy. Yet they survived. Was this because the Almighty Lord had willed it? Or was this simply an example of life's mysteries?

He wondered if trying to hold off the enemy was a sensible thing to do. By creating this wall of resistance so that others could escape, he was placing his men at risk. What guarantee was there that anyone would ever make it to freedom? For all his good intentions, they could all be slain.

While Malko pondered this thought, the moment he feared arrived.

A faint, dark, low-hanging cloud was seen moving slowly towards them in the distance, getting larger and growing more menacing the closer it came to

Shamash. In the very far distance, Malko saw smoke curling into the sky where there were once villages. Malko sent a messenger to alert the others. Within minutes, word spread from house to house, and the roofs filled with armed men and boys ready to fight to death.

Malko spotted a man in the lead racing towards the village at top speed. He was leaning close to his horse, his cape flapping in the wind; together they resembled some prehistoric beast from hell in flight. The man's free arm could be seen under his flying cape, signaling his men to ride faster. "Death to the infidels!" he shouted, his voice rising above the sound of galloping horses.

"*Death to the infidels*," his men repeated in thunderous unison.

Malko waited for the right moment to begin firing. Given the size of the army rushing towards Shamash, he knew he could never stop the enemy. What he saw ahead was a thick, impenetrable wall made up of endless rows of men who were swiftly closing in on them.

Malko suspected that there would be no way he and his men would be able to survive this attack. The enemy's numbers far exceeded the size and capabilities of Malko's modest arsenal.

His only hope was to be able to delay them long enough for all those seeking shelter at the mission or in Russia to reach safety. His faith – and the possibility that by some miracle of God they might survive – saved him from giving up, throwing his gun down, and yielding to defeat.

Malko silently said a short prayer, an earthly goodbye, and aimed his gun. When the moment was right, he released the first shot; as planned, it was followed by an explosion of fire from all the other rooftops. After that well-timed burst of fire, the enemy began to fall to the ground, where they were trampled by the horses, turning the snow the color of blood.

"*Jihad!*" the leader shouted. "*Allāhu Akbar.*"

"*Jihad!*" his men shouted back, waving guns and sabers in the air. "*Allāhu Akbar.*"

At almost the precise moment when the enemy was approaching from the west, another enemy appeared from behind, coming from the east. It was the enemy who lived among them: the Persian Mohammedans who rose up from nowhere again, after waiting patiently for this precise moment to attack.

Chapter 16

The American Mission, Urmia

The Mission Gatekeeper heard gunshots outside the walled city. For the past few days, he had heard very little else. Although deeply concerned about what was happening, Tamzi knew better than to check. The Turks were in control and they were showing no mercy. After one particularly disturbing incident, punctuated by horrendous cries of pain, he couldn't control himself any longer. He climbed to the top of the twenty-foot wall surrounding the mission to peek outside. What he saw beyond the wall was a sea of people trying to push their way into the city. Some of them were pulled aside and shot and tossed into the moat surrounding the city; others were being stripped of their possessions before being allowed to enter Urmia.

A soldier outside the city saw the Gatekeeper peeking over the wall and aimed his rifle at him. *"Get back in!"* he commanded, "or I'll blast your head off."

Tamzi immediately descended to safety. He wondered how long the thousands of Christians who were sheltered in the mission would be safe.

There was a prevailing fear that at any given moment the Kurds and the Turks would push their way into the compound and slaughter them. The responsibility for preventing this lay on him.

Each time he opened the massive door to let someone in, he worried. The pressure to carefully screen the hundreds of refugees seeking asylum before admitting them was enormous. One mistake, one wrong decision, and he could be overpowered by looters and murderers. His only hope that this wouldn't occur was the American flag. As long as it flew above the walled mission, as long as the Americans remained neutral during the war, the refugees were safe and allowed to live within the compound without fear of being slaughtered. But if this neutrality should ever be broken, if the Americans changed their war position by taking sides with the Allies, anything could happen, and there would be no one – no force strong enough – to prevent it.

Since the line of communication with the outside world was broken, he and everyone else at the mission lived in isolation, without access to current news reports on the war movement. No one knew what the Americans were planning. They didn't even know if the cables they sent to other missions to ask for assistance were received. Without any communication with the outside world, Tamzi lived in the dark, surrounded by a belligerent foe totally lacking in scruples, whom he constantly had to try to outwit.

Seeing all these people arrive daily – stripped of their possessions, begging for admission – was often more than he could handle emotionally. Sometimes he had to look aside because he found the sight of their wounds or their suffering too upsetting.

Many of the refugees traveled great distances to reach Urmia. They came in small groups; the lucky ones arrived on donkey-driven carts belonging to Mohammedans who took pity on them. Most of them just staggered to the mission gate with little more than the rags they wore. What worldly possessions they brought with them were given up at the gates of Urmia and claimed by the *askars* and other Turkish soldiers who greedily stole whatever they could before allowing anyone to enter the city.

Those who were lucky enough to make it to the mission told Tamzi outrageous stories of cruelty and abuse – old people used as latrines, young girls successively dishonored in front of their terrified parents, and infants being bayonetted. They told him heartbreaking stories of a world crushed by lawlessness and carnage, with homes robbed and burned, and men butchered, all because of their religious beliefs. The horror the refugees collectively spoke about broke loose, and a cry of pain rose up to heaven in one pitiful, dissonant wail, the moment they were safe at the mission.

Women beat their breasts with their fists and scratched their faces with their nails as they told Tamzi their personal stories. One young woman told him how she had escaped death by hiding in a well. When she finally surfaced after everyone left, she saw bodies everywhere. Many were mutilated beyond recognition.

"Everywhere I turned I saw a river of blood," she said to Tamzi, "When I reached the gates of Urmia the *askars* and the Turkish soldiers guarding the gates took what little I had left – my shoes, my coat, and anything else of value. They said it was a war levy, which I had to pay, if I didn't want to get shot."

Others told of scavengers weaving through the crowd at the gates, posing as friends, who had promised the Christians they would hide their valuables from the *askars* until it was safe for them to reclaim their possessions.

"A few people gave them what they had," one woman said. "Some actually believed that the scavengers would return it one day."

At night, when the city gates were closed and Urmia was asleep, it wasn't unusual for the Gatekeeper to be awakened by the pounding at the door. Each time he heard it, he feared this could be the moment he dreaded. Tonight could be the night when an army of Turks would decide to take control of the mission. Frightened, he would dress quickly and head to the gate. Without opening it, he would cautiously call to the other side.

"Identify yourself. Who wishes to awaken me at this hour of the night?"

"I'm the Turk Mareşal," a man shouted. "Open this gate immediately."

"It's late. Everyone's asleep. You must come back in the morning."

"Are you defying my command?"

"What do you want that is so important that you must disturb us at this hour?"

"I want a girl. I understand you have some for sale, and I need one for my men."

"This is an American mission. We have no girls for sale."

"I command you. Open this gate immediately. I must see for myself."

"I am sorry. I cannot let you in."

"How dare you disobey the command of a Turkish officer."

"I fear, sir, your request is unreasonable. Come back in the morning. Goodnight."

A blast of fire was heard outside the mission gate. A bullet pierced the thick wooden door and lodged itself in it at the exit point. If the bullet had made its way completely through the massive door, he would have been hit in the stomach. On the other side of the gate, a man cussed in Arabic; this outburst was followed by silence.

The following day the Gatekeeper faced another incident, which might have been the result of the late night disturbance. A group of Turkish soldiers arrived with their commanding officer and requested the right to search the grounds.

"I have no authority to permit this," Tamzi said.

"Then get someone with authority," the Officer said.

The Gatekeeper dispatched a boy to find Reverend Michael Johnson.

"What can I do for you?" the Reverend nervously asked the Officer when he arrived.

"I am looking for criminals," the Officer said.

"We have no criminals here. This is a mission."

"I have heard otherwise, that you are harboring blue eyes among the Christians."

"Blue eyes?" the Reverend asked, confused.

"Russian spies."

"You are mistaken. There are no Russian spies here."

"We wish to see for ourselves."

Terrified of the consequences of denying them access to the compound, the Reverend took them on a tour of the property.

When they left, the Reverend relaxed.

"Thank the Lord that's over," he said to Tamzi.

"Did they find anything?" Tamzi asked.

"Nothing, of course," the Reverend replied. "I think they were looking for guns… not Russians."

"Guns? We don't have guns. Where would they get such an idea?"

"They're probably just being cautious," the Reverend said. "I think they're worried the Christians might rise up and take arms against them."

Abigail assumed the role of the matriarch of the family and took full command of all activities and decisions. Being in control gave her the strength to continue. As long as she led, she could function without yielding to self-pity.

Her first challenge as the leader of the family was to set up a sleeping schedule. The only space that the Reverend could spare for the family was a small, box-shaped chamber in the physicians' residence next to the hospital. Because of the limited space, no one in the family was able to sleep lying down. Instead, they had to sleep back to back or against the wall. Abigail's solution was simple and sensible. Since the needs at the mission were around the clock, and since each member of the family and staff was called to assist in one way or another at different times of the day, she arranged a sleeping schedule for everyone that suited their work schedule. While one group was assisting at the hospital or in the kitchen, the other group slept. This provided them all with enough space for a comfortable rest.

No one among the Shamash group dared to complain. Abigail saw to it by reminding them how privileged they were to have this entire room for themselves while the other refugees had to huddle together in halls or in storage areas.

Because of the thousands of people seeking shelter at the mission, each day the family faced new problems, which required their full attention. This allowed them very little time to complain. The most urgent problem was dealing with all the dead bodies. Many of the refugees arrived at the mission with diseases brought on by poor hygiene or malnutrition or contact with vermin. To reduce the danger of an out-of-control epidemic, Abigail recommended that the sick be separated from the others until they recovered, and that all corpses be disposed of right away. Since the frozen earth was too hard to break in order to bury the dead properly, Abigail put together a team of workers who would collect the bodies, pile them in heaps, and cremate them to avoid the spread of any disease.

The scavengers hired to remove the bodies and the human waste on donkey carts often refused to enter the commons. The smell from the decaying bodies and the human waste was too offensive for them to tolerate. As a result, a cloudy stench of human waste and burning flesh hovered over the compound and seeped into the buildings and the earth. Combined, it was like nothing familiar, a mix of the putrid and the beefy, the nauseating and the sweet. One whiff was sufficient to be remembered for a lifetime.

Abigail didn't know how long she could manage. As long as she didn't think about it too much, she was fine, but the moment she paused long enough to observe all the suffering around her, she would panic. When she was alone, she did the only thing she could do. She got on her knees and prayed.

"Dear Lord, please give me the strength to continue. I feel so helpless alone. And please, *please* Dear Lord bring back Malko safely. I so need him."

Nothing prepared Judith for what was happening. As terrifying as her kidnapping had been, it could never compare to this. At least when she was kidnapped Judith knew that if she escaped from her abductors and made it home, it would be over, and she would be safe again. Now, though, there was no home to run to; no dolls, no Sag, and no comfortable place to go to forget. Stripped of her private world of privilege, she was thrust into the raw presence without an exit. Helpless, she watched as her old world disappeared. A fierce and wild new world began to emerge in its place, turning her past into a historical footnote.

Her new home had become a crowded, vermin-infested corner of the world, where she survived with her family, surrounded by thousands of desperate people. To tolerate what she saw happening, she encircled herself with a protective shield. Judith watched the injured being led to the hospital, leaving behind a stream of blood, and felt nothing. She heard women crying in agony as their loved ones were cremated, and she didn't understand. Everywhere she turned, it was the same. Words and action, devoid for her of emotional and intellectual connection.

When the sights became too grim to observe, Judith locked herself in the kitchen with Leah, where she would hide in the past. While working in the kitchen, where the unpleasant smell of death was masked by the agreeable aroma of baking bread, Judith felt as though she were at Shamash again, away from the tragic and the morbid, safe in the familiar and the comfortable.

During one of her escapes into the past, her mother made an unexpected visit to the kitchen to see her.

"Look, Mamma," Judith said, rolling out the dough for the bread. "I can make *kada* all by myself. Leah taught me. Isn't that wonderful?"

"Yes, *ma petite*, it is wonderful."

"Why don't you get Grandmamma? I want to show her how easily I prepare bread."

"Later, dear. She's resting now."

"That's all she does lately. Is she all right, Mamma?" she asked, concerned.

"She's fine. She's just taking a short rest in the hospital."

"In the hospital!"

"It's okay. The doctors promise she'll be out in a few days."

"My grandmamma's in the hospital?"

"That's right, Judith. That's what I said."

Judith remembered all the people she saw being cremated. Was her grandmamma going to be one of them? Would she be like all the others tossed into a heap and burned to ashes? The thought of her grandmamma disappearing into a cloud of smoke was more than Judith could bear. Her protective shield shattered, relieving her of any emotional isolation. For one violent moment, she felt the razor-sharp edge of pain. Like the hymn says, *she saw the storm*.

Judith panicked. "My grandmamma isn't going to die, is she, Mamma? Tell me, Mamma, honestly. Grandmamma's not going to die?"

"No, Judith. The doctor assured me. She'll be fine after a little rest."

"Take me to her, Mamma. I want to see her."

"Later, Judith."

"But I want to see her now."

"Judith, it would be best for you to wait. She needs her rest."

"I don't want to wait. I want to see my grandmamma."

"Judith, be reasonable."

Judith was no longer listening to her mother. Everything changed for her, panic and fear took over. She ran from her mother's side to the hospital ward. The minute she entered she could feel the presence of death. Beds were lined parallel on both sides of the long, narrow room. Nurses were in motion, going from bed to bed, checking the temperature, feeling the pulse, and bandaging the wounds. Judith hurried down the row of beds until she located her grandmother; Miriam was lying in bed lifelessly with her mouth and eyes half open. Judith collapsed to her knees beside her grandmother.

"Grandmamma, it's Judith. Can you hear me, Grandmamma?"

Miriam's hand slipped from the covers and fell alongside the bed, where Judith took hold of it. It was quivering and hot, so hot that it worried Judith.

"Judith," Miriam said weakly, "you've come."

"Yes, Grandmamma."

She gave Judith's hand a gentle squeeze. "Why aren't you at school? You should be at school today."

"There is no school today, Grandmamma."

"Is today a holiday?"

"No, Grandmamma. We are at war."

"That's right," Miriam said as though her mental haze had suddenly lifted, freeing her of any temporary confusion. "I forgot."

"Please get well, Grandmamma. For my sake, please."

Her grandmother's frail voice was difficult to hear over the commotion in the ward. Judith had to move closer and listen hard.

"I can't," her grandmother whispered. "I must leave. The Lord is calling."

"Tell Him to wait." She kissed her grandmother's quivering hand. "I don't want you to leave me."

"You mustn't worry, my child. You won't be alone. I've asked the Lord to watch over you."

"Please, Grandmamma. Ask Him for just a little more time. I beg you."

"There's no more time left, Judith. My time has come. But He did tell me to leave you something."

"I don't want anything, Grandmamma. I just want you."

"It's something you always wanted."

"I told you, Grandmamma. I don't want anything. I just want you to get better."

"But it's the brooch of Shamash."

Judith pressed her face against her grandmother's hand and began to cry. "I told you. I don't want anything. I just want you, Grandmamma. That's all."

"Take it, my darling. You may need it one day."

"Why is this happening, Grandmamma?" Judith asked, confused. "Why are we all being punished like this?"

"You must put your trust in the Lord," Miriam said weakly. "He alone will bring you understanding."

Her mother, who was standing silently beside her daughter, spoke suddenly. "Come, Judith," Abigail said. "It's time for your grandmother to rest."

Judith rose reluctantly. "I'll be back, Grandmamma," she said. "I'll be back. I promise." Her grandmother didn't respond; she merely stared at the ceiling with half-open eyes.

Judith watched the snow fall steadily on the porch of the physician's quarters, adding another layer to what had already fallen during the night. Near her, protected from the snow, hidden under covers, were rows of refugees, pressed against each other for warmth.

This can't be the end. Grandmamma will get better, she kept telling herself. *Dear God, please make her better.* Judith was crying and hurting inside in a way she had never hurt or cried before. Why was this all happening? *Oh dear Lord, why did you let the Russians leave us? Please bring them back. I plead with you.*

Please bring them back so that we can all return safely to Shamash.

Judith was standing on the porch, praying silently, when she heard someone call her name.

"Judith," the voice said. "Is that you?"

She turned towards the voice. Standing in the snow, almost completely disguised by the white flakes that covered him, was the Sardar. His blue eyes were sparkling like evening stars. Frightened by the sight of him, Judith backed away, tripping over someone's feet behind her. She quickly recovered her balance by grabbing the porch railing.

"Don't come near me," she said.

He stepped closer. "I won't harm you. I just came to see you if you were all right."

"I'll scream. I'll scream my head off if you come closer."

"Don't you want me to take you and your family away from this?"

"We don't want anything from you."

"But you'll be safer with me. You won't be hungry anymore. Look at yourself, how filthy you are, how skinny you've become. With me, there would be no more sickness and starvation, no more want. Wouldn't you and your family like that?"

He was tempting her with promises to corrupt her. Wasn't that what the serpent did in the Garden of Eden? Judith resisted. "I don't want anything from you," she said, frightened. "Get away from me. You had me kidnapped. You killed Sag. *I hate you!*"

"Don't reject me, Judith. You can have anything you want. Just come with me."

She looked at him – through him. How could she trust anyone who believed in a God that caused others so much grief? Life with him wouldn't be any different than it was for Sadina with Ghulam. She could never accept his domination; she could never give up her freedom for just a little comfort.

"I don't trust you," Judith said bitterly. "You're an evil man. Stay away from me."

"What must I do to convince you you're wrong? Ask for anything, and I will deliver."

"I don't want anything from you. It all has a price, which I'm not willing to pay."

A child's pitiful cry for help unexpectedly interrupted the conversation. A girl half Judith's age – shoeless, wearing a thin dress, shivering – was standing near Judith, reaching out to a woman who hurried past her.

"Mamma," she said tearfully, "is that you? It's Dina."

The woman was so self-absorbed that she didn't notice the child. A man came from behind the girl and in his haste knocked the girl aside. The girl raised her voice desperately in an effort to be heard above the confusion.

"It's Dina, Mamma." the girl shouted. "Can't you hear me?"

Overcome by emotion, Judith hurried past the Governor to the girl, whom she quickly hid inside her woolen coat.

"Come with me," Judith said in a comforting tone. "Let me help you find your mamma."

The girl looked up at Judith with sad and trusting brown eyes and yielded without a whimper while Judith led her quickly into the warm hospital compound.

The Shamash Village

The Turks and the Kurds broke through the barricaded doors of the Shamash house and began to kill the survivors systematically. Malko bravely stood at the foot of the stairs leading to the roof, and aimed his rifle at the enemy who dared to climb the steps. Standing there, looming above them against the daylight, Malko was both an easy target and a menacing adversary – until he unexpectedly felt the sharp pain of a bullet. He instantly dropped his gun and tumbled down the stairs, rolling over dead bodies along the way.

He was dragged into the courtyard, where others were lined up, and left to rest in the snow. All around him he saw death, bodies hacked into pieces and smashed beyond recognition.

Malko spotted a man, wrapped in a cape, whom his soldiers called Ejder. He was looking over the survivors with a grin of evil amusement. "Where are the women?" he asked an old man backed against the wall. The man was silent. Ejder pointed the tip of his saber at the man's throat. "Speak," he commanded.

The man trembled at the touch of the saber. "They've left. All of them. That's all I know."

"Yes, but where, Old Man? Tell me," Ejder's voice grew uglier, "or I'll slice off your head."

"I don't know anything," the man said, frightened. "Honest!"

"Where?"

"I told you. I don't know," he said, breaking into tears.

"Liar," Ejder said; he then swung his saber across the man's neck with all his might. The man's head rolled across the ground, while his body collapsed lifelessly. Ejder approached the next man, then pointed his saber at the man's throat.

"Where are the women?"

The man stared, horrified, at the headless body on the ground.

"Speak, you swine," Ejder said. He pricked the man's neck with the tip of his saber and drew blood. "Where are the women?"

"In Urmia," the man said, trembling, as he looked into Ejder's wild eyes.

"Where in Urmia?" Ejder asked.

"I don't know."

"Liar," Ejder shouted and slashed off his head too. He spotted an adolescent boy, whom he eyed with familiarity. "Come here, boy," he said.

Frightened, the boy moved hesitatingly towards Ejder, his head bowed. Ejder turned the boy around a few times, carefully examining him. "Not bad," he said, and he shoved the boy towards a soldier.

"Take him inside. Show him how to please the men."

"You have one last chance," Ejder said to the remaining Christians lined against the wall. "Say *shahada* and you'll live." There was silence. "Repeat after me," he commanded, his voice rising to a dangerous pitch. "*Ash-hadu an la ilaha ill Allah*. There are no gods worthy of worship except Allah." No one responded. He eyed them furiously. "Are you refusing to forsake your God?"

They all began to sing together.

My heart is aching, I see the storm;
All around me, the ocean roars.
Give me strength, my Lord, to make it home;
For all around me, I see the storm.

"Shoot them," Ejder commanded. The singing continued until the last person was dead.

Malko couldn't bear watching his courtyard turn into a slaughterhouse. He turned his head towards a parade of people hurrying from his home, some of whom he recognized. They were his Mohammedan neighbors, whom he knew well. Until this moment, he had had no reason to doubt the sincerity of their friendship. Seeing them remove from his home everything that was portable and of value – from rugs to silver – left him wondering how long they had waited for this moment to strip him of his heritage. Several of them glanced at him, but quickly looked away when they saw he was still alive. As he lay on the ground feeling the pain of his wound travel through his body, he watched as all his family treasures were moved past him and out of the gate in the courtyard.

After the last villager was shot and pulverized with clubs, Ejder turned his attention to the last three men remaining, the three publishers of the *Zahria-d-Bahra* whom he had saved for the end. "For you, my three illustrious leaders," Ejder said, "I have something special."

He addressed a man in a green turban and a black robe, pointing to Daniel, Issac and Malko. "Take them, Sayid," he said. "They're yours."

Malko felt the cold hand of death rest upon him. He knew what would follow. It was the habit of these savages to separate the leaders and give them special treatment – a painful and ritualistic death.

The Sayid removed a knife from his leather case. Daniel was the first to be selected for execution. He was held in place by two men while the Sayid took his hand and surgically removed each finger.

"Don't," Malko cried out, dragging himself towards Daniel. "Take me, let him be. Please let him be." Ejder came up to Malko and stepped on his back, pinning him against the cold snow.

"*Allāhu akbar!*" the Sayid said jubilantly after cutting off each of Daniel's fingers. He then cut off Daniel's hand. "*Allāhu akbar!*" he repeated to heaven. "God is great!"

Pinned to the cold snow, Malko helplessly stretched an arm towards Daniel. "Don't, please.

Show him pity. He is an old man. For God's sake, can't you be a little more merciful?"

In agony, bleeding profusely, Daniel cried out to him, "Forgive them, my son. They know not what they do" To silence Daniel, the Sayid signaled a soldier to step forward. While Daniel was bleeding and wrestling with his pain, the soldier crushed his head with a huge club.

The Sayid took this moment to wipe his knife clean and prepare for the next execution.

This ritual was repeated exactly the same way with Issac. When it was Malko's turn and the Sayid was ready to begin his execution, a voice was heard unexpectedly. "*Stop!* That one's mine."

The American Mission

While Judith trudged through the snow, carrying bread from the kitchen to the infirmary, she saw the Governor walk towards her, and she shuddered. His henchman was pulling a cart from which an arm and a leg were hanging.

"Judith," the Governor called. "I have something for you."

Judith hesitated at approaching the Governor, who loomed before her, a diabolic creation disguised magnificently with beautiful features. A voice within her told her to hurry back to the kitchen and wait for him to leave. But she couldn't move. She just remained in place, a frozen statue carrying a basket of bread.

"Don't you want to see your father?" the Governor asked.

"Daddy?" Judith dropped her loaves of bread and hurried to the cart. She cried out with joy when she saw her father stretched out inside the cart. "Daddy, are you all right? Speak to me, Daddy, it's Judith."

He opened his eyes slowly, vaguely staring in her direction. "Judith…?"

"Yes, Daddy."

He smiled, lifted his arm with great effort, and stroked her cheek gently. "I've come home, Judith. Your daddy has come home."

Chapter 17

The American Mission, Spring

At last, Jonathan Peterson felt safe shopping in the market without hiring an *askar*. The fear of being kidnapped by a Kurd and held for ransom was no longer a concern. The Kurds who enjoyed preying on vulnerable missionaries like Jonathan were fleeing the city. Left behind were the Turkish soldiers diligently cleaning up the area. With the departure of the Kurds and many of the Turks, there came a renewed energy, the energy of a new season that brought with it the promise of hope.

Spring arrived. Flowers were popping up everywhere; trees and bushes began to bud. Each day Jonathan returned from his shopping trip with good news. Unlike in winter, he no longer complained about the artificially high prices he had to pay for basic foods. All the food prices were dropping, slowly returning to their pre-war levels. Although he was able to buy more of what the mission needed than before, Jonathan still wasn't able to buy enough to feed everyone sufficiently. So much of their money had been taken by the Turks during the winter; this had left the mission with very little cash. What credit that was extended to them by some of the merchants was almost completely exhausted.

Still, this didn't worry Jonathan. Rumors were circulating in the marketplace that the Russians were returning. This was confirmed by a noticeable reduction of the Turkish military in the city, and reconfirmed by the sudden disappearance of the gallows that had been erected by the city gates for hanging anyone unable to pay their war levy. Such news traveled through the mission swiftly, and it provided the sick and hungry with the courage to persevere.

When Jonathan returned to the mission after shopping, a man wearing rags infinitely too large for his frame approached him. Reduced to a skeleton, the man was one of the many refugees who were braving the stench of human waste saturating the mission grounds, solely for the pleasure of resting in the warm afternoon sun. "Is it true about the Turks?" he asked. "Are they really leaving?"

Jonathan smiled. "That's only part of the good news."

"There's more?" the man asked excitedly.

"Much more."

"Tell me everything. I want to hear it all."

"There's too much to tell. So I'll be brief," he said, his voice rising with joy. "The Russians defeated the Turks in the Caucasus…."

"*Hallelujah!*"

"…and thousands of Turkish soldiers died during the cold winter without a shot being fired."

"*Praise the Lord!*"

"What about the Pasha? Was he one of them?"

"No," Jonathan said sadly, "he retreated to Constantinople before the Russians could get him."

"Are the Russians returning to the Plain?"

"That's what I hear."

"Thank God," the man said jubilantly, "our prayers have been answered."

The Return of the Russians

Celebratory music and dancing filled the streets. Abigail observed the excitement, when she and her family stepped from the mission compound to observe the Russians enter Urmia through one of the main gates of the city. The heavy cloud of despair that had hovered over the Plain lifted. Life resumed again, and the possibilities for the future seemed infinite.

"Look! The Russians have arrived!" the crowd was shouting as the military procession entered the city on horseback and began traveling slowly along the narrow, winding streets of Urmia. When the soldiers waved to the crowd, they were showered with flowers and cheers. "Praise the Lord! You've returned safely!"

Abigail watched as girls abandoned all convention and allowed the young Russian soldiers to sweep them up into their arms and carry them away on horseback like lovers united after a long separation.

Although Abigail wasn't caught up in the excitement of the moment, she still enjoyed the procession with a melancholy smile. After all the pain she and her family had endured as a result of the war, Abigail was still burdened by the lingering memory of what she had experienced. For her, this long-awaited good fortune was only a brief interruption to her grief.

"I wonder how long this euphoria will last," Malko said to Abigail.

"We mustn't think that far ahead," Abigail said in an attempt to enjoy the excitement of the moment. "Let's just be thankful, Malko, that they're back and we can go home again."

The horses which had transported the Shamash family to the mission were no longer available. They had been sold to the Turks for food and medical supplies during the winter. Life had to go on, and like so many other families, the Shamashes had to make decisions. As the ragged remains of her family began their long walk home, Abigail wondered what would await them at Shamash.

En route home, they passed the ruins of what had once been prosperous and happy Christian villages; all of them had been gutted by fire, reduced to shells, and exposed for view by broken walls. Whatever small joy freedom brought her was painfully interrupted by the sight of the wasted villages, and the body parts scattered along the road or floating in the river.

As she watched Malko withdraw into himself at the sight of this destruction, Abigail realized that her mighty warrior was dying before her. His near-death experience defending Shamash had changed him. Everything he saw seemed to bring him tears and sorrow.

He had recovered from the gunshot wound, she thought, but he had lost his spirit. Seeing him broken upset her. During all their years together, he had always been the strength of the family, but since the battle of Shamash, and the murder of his two dearest friends, he had changed. While struggling to survive in the mission with the others, he kept worrying about the future. How would they ever live, when he was sure everything they had was gone? Losing his wealth was something he couldn't handle. He never knew a life without money. With everything gone and nothing of value remaining, he would have to figure out a way to begin all over.

"How will we live?" he repeatedly asked Abigail. *"How will we ever make it?"*

"We mustn't worry about that, Malko," she said. "We must take one day at a time. The Lord will take care of the rest."

He shook his head, as though he were rejecting this, as he slipped into his thoughts.

"I'm so looking forward to being home again," Abigail said, trying to engage him in conversation, as they walked to Shamash. "It will be so nice to plant my vegetables and enjoy some of Leah's yoghurt-spinach soup. Won't that be a nice treat?"

"Yes, dear," he said in a distant voice. "That'll be very nice."

"Do you think any of our fruit trees will produce? I would give anything for some of Leah's marmalade."

"Yes, Abigail," he said, still lost in his emotional fog. "I agree."

Abigail gave up trying to engage him in conversation, and she just walked beside him silently, hand-in-hand. His mind was on a journey, and he wasn't ready to talk.

Judith unexpectedly shrieked. She was staring at the broken arm of what seemed to be a baby. Tears streamed down her face. Abigail put her arms around Judith, hugging her tightly. "Don't stare, *chérie*," she said. "This is no time for tears. Later, when we are safe, we can look back together. In the meantime, we must be strong!"

Although the orchards and wooded areas belonging to the Christians were destroyed, the Mohammedan communities thrived, untouched by the invasion. Some of their non-Christian neighbors waved to the Shamashes when they passed. Others just ignored them and busied themselves with their work. Nothing had changed for the Mohammedans. Their villages were as before, and the women were performing their usual tasks – washing the clothes by the river shore and porting well water home on their shoulders.

One of their Mohammedan neighbors, obviously startled to see Malko, greeted him on the road. He was a long-time friend who had spent hours in conversation with Malko about land management. The man embraced Malko, but Malko pulled back.

"You've survived," Akbar said, surprised. "I wasn't sure what had happened to you after they destroyed your village."

"We're fine," Malko said politely.

"And the Reverend, is he fine too?"

Malko's eyes filled with tears. The question triggered memories. "Martyred," he said simply.

"I'm sorry," Akbar said.

Abigail changed the subject, filling her voice with a sonorous joy. "How's your family, Akbar? Fine, I hope."

"Oh yes, we're all doing fine," he said, "Why don't you come over and join us for dinner. We can talk together at length."

"That's very kind," Malko said, "but…"

"No excuses," Akbar insisted. "It would bring the entire family great pleasure to see you all again."

Malko yielded, more out of courtesy than pleasure. She could tell by his attitude towards his friend that something was seriously wrong. Malko was creating a distance between him and Akbar, which had never happened before. When they entered Akbar's village, everything was as before, peaceful and quiet, completely undisturbed by the war. As Abigail enjoyed the tea and meze, which Akbar's wife had prepared for the Shamash family, she heard her favorite clock, which once belonged to her grandfather, chime the hour. Gazing about Akbar's small house, Abigail began to notice many of their other possessions in the room. She glanced at Malko and made a gesture with her head towards an oriental rug. He responded by nodding his head to inform her that he noticed it as well.

"You are very fortunate to be alive," Akbar said. "Many of your people weren't so lucky."

"Yes, it's true," Abigail said. "God has been kind to us and spared us."

"Your mother," he said to Abigail. "She is fine too, I hope."

Abigail bit her lip in an effort to hold back the emotion; she shook her head. "Typhoid."

"I am so sorry to hear that. She will be greatly missed," Akbar said. "She was always such a gracious lady. At least, you and the rest of your family are safe. Thanks be to Allah for that."

Abigail noted that his words were carefully selected to convey the right sentiment, but to her they all seemed shallow, without any sincere feeling. She wondered why Akbar had invited them to his house. Was it to flaunt his theft of their property, or was it a genuine act of kindness? She didn't know. She didn't care. She saw him differently now; Malko obviously did as well. He was no longer a trusted neighbor and a friend, but an opportunist who benefited from their misfortune.

When Abigail and her family returned to Shamash, they were greeted by the bodies of villagers, scattered everywhere, reduced to bones. Seeing them instantly brought tears to her eyes.

All their animals were gone and their fields were scorched. But a few spring flowers were miraculously breaking through the ash-colored earth. They were like colorful dots of beauty that added relief to the otherwise depressing setting. Abigail picked a few of them, brought them close to her chest, and enjoyed their fresh fragrance. She found a glass that survived the battle, filled it with water, and placed the flowers in it.

She stared at them sadly. "Life always manages to continue even among the ashes."

Malko wasn't listening. He was surveying the land and making note of all the body parts around him. He obviously faced his own demons. "Nothing's left," he said sadly. "Everything and everyone, gone."

"We'll just have to begin again," she said encouragingly.

"Why? So those pigs can repeat their crime?"

"That needn't be the case, Malko. The Russians are back. We're safe again."

"For how long?"

"Malko, please. We mustn't think so far ahead. Day-by-day, it's better that way."

"Tell me honestly, Abigail, do you want to spend the rest of your life living day-by-day, uncertain of what will happen next? What about Judith's safety? Can we afford to remain so close to the Governor? He is a man obsessed. He won't give up until he snatches Judith from us."

"Do you want to leave, Malko? Is that what you want?"

He nodded.

Looking about at what remained, she had no desire to stay. It was time for them to move on. There
was nothing left to salvage.

"Very well, Malko. That's what we'll do – leave."

A spark of life returned to his expression. "I will
start planning. We can form a caravan to Hamadan
and follow the English south to freedom."

"What about money?" she asked. "We will need
money for our passage."

"Of course," Malko said. "How stupid of me to
forget. We'll need money. Plenty of it."

He bolted to the rear of the house. She quickly
followed him. "Where are you going?"

"To the stables, Abigail," he said. "That's where I
buried the gold."

Using a shovel he had found on the ground, he
feverishly began to dig next to the boulder near what
remained of the apricot tree.

"It's here," he said when the shovel struck metal.
"The chest is here. We are free, Abigail. Free to *live*
again."

Judith bit her lip to hold back the pain. On the
walls of the main hall, written in huge, red letters,
were the words, "Praise be to Allah, Death to the
Infidels." Seeing each letter made with what appeared to be blood, she thought of her grandfather
and all the other village men and boys she had
once known and who were now dead, and she
wondered whose blood had been used to write
those words. The thought was too morbid for her

to bear – just thinking about it brought tears of outrage to her. She climbed the steps to her bedroom, dreading what might await her.

En route to her room, she saw that all the family possessions that had once made it a home were gone. There was no furniture or paintings or rugs – or even Sag – to welcome her. All the rooms were stripped of valuables. What was left was either broken or shredded and scattered on the floor. Her bedroom door had been broken by force, and it lay flat on the floor for her to step over. Nothing remained in her room except her religious dolls, which had been smashed and heaped in a pile. Those made of cloth had been shredded with a knife. Hidden amongst them was the Queen of Sheba – a little soiled, but otherwise intact. Judith pulled it from the pile and brought it close to her, cuddling it in her arms. She remembered the man at the bazaar and her foolish greed, and the Governor and Sag – but most of all, she remembered her grandmother. All these memories collected together and released themselves in a deep, sorrowful sob.

The Governor's Mansion, Summer

Any dream which the Governor might have secretly nurtured of claiming the Peacock Throne faded with the Turks' defeat in the Caucasus. Demir Pasha's plan to reclaim the area by destroying the Russians' stronghold was a military blunder which forced him to return to Constantinople in disgrace. Once again the Governor was back where he had started. The

Russians were in power in the Plain, and the surviving Christians had returned to reclaim their land. As before, he had to yield to the superior political powers and become a diplomat, and friend to all. Such was the nature of his job – such was the nature of survival. Years of living by his wit, without a large family fortune to protect him, had left the Governor weary and discouraged. Just when he thought he was ready to snatch prosperity, his opportunity was taken away from him.

At least he had been wise enough to take some of the antiquities and books in Malko's library, especially the priceless fifteenth-century religious painting of the three apostles. The Governor immediately recognized its monetary value, overlooking its religious reference. After the war, he would take it and the other things he had acquired to Europe, where he hoped to sell them at a handsome price. To safeguard them while they were in his possession, the Governor kept them at home, in a private chamber to which only he had access.

There was only one other thing left to claim, and that was Judith. She was an obsession of which he couldn't free himself. The more she eluded him, the more important she became. His need for her was greater than any sexual desire. It was a fundamental need that touched the very essence of all man-woman relationships. It was his need to reduce that proud Assyrian princess to wifely servitude.

Somehow he had to devise a way to take her. He knew it could never be achieved using any traditional method, because she would stubbornly resist. To the Governor's disappointment, saving Malko didn't bring the response he had sought. Judith had made no effort to convey her appreciation – beyond a thank you – for what he had done. Undoubtedly, she was smart enough to see through him and identify his act of humanitarian kindness for what it was: an attempt to manipulate her. To claim Judith, he would have to set up circumstance that would provide her with no choice but to yield to his will.

While the Governor was pondering his next move, his servant entered with the latest news from the nearby villages.

"Sardar Jamshih, the Christians are leaving," he said to the Governor.

"What are you talking about?" the Governor asked, startled.

"It has just come to my attention that a caravan of Christians is heading south."

"But why? The Russians have returned. They are safe again. Why would they care to leave?"

"I don't know, Sardar."

"What about the Shamash family?" he asked in a sudden burst of panic. "Have they left too?"

"I don't know that either."

"You're useless! I need information, and you bring me nothing." The Governor pushed his way past his servant. "Get out of my way, *swine!*" He left the room in a flurry of movement.

In the courtyard of the Shamash home, there was no sign of death. The bodies left behind after the mass murder of men and boys had been removed and buried in what had once been a very fertile orchard. Wooden crosses were placed at the burial spot to mark the site.

The large house on the edge of the river that over-looked the village stood exactly as the Governor had last seen it. There were the same broken doors and windows, bullet holes and bloodstain writings on the walls. But despite all this disfigurement, the house still stood intact, graceful and solid, a reminder to others that it had once belonged to a very pros-perous and important family.

He entered the house and looked about. There was no sign that Judith had ever lived here. It was just another great house in the Plain that was deserted and vandalized.

In what was once Judith's room, he saw the broken pieces of her dolls, crushed with a blunt instrument and heaped in one corner of the room. He buried his face in his hands and wept. "She's gone," he cried. "My Judith has left me."

The Caravan to Baghdad

Judith wasn't the same person she had been before the war. Little by little, she was changing. Some-times she didn't recognize herself. She was no longer the young girl who used to romp outside with Sag, or wear pretty dresses with silk bows and sashes, and dance and recite poems. She had become another girl, someone more guarded, *less* trusting; more sensitive, *less* innocent. Hanging over her heavily was a cloud of sadness which she couldn't push aside. She had seen too much and felt too much pain. The charmed world which she had once known was gone forever, leaving her with a vague memory and an ever-present fear that what she knew now could disappear as well.

Wearing pretty dresses and covering her body with floral perfume no longer appealed to her. The last thing Judith wanted to do was make herself attractive again; she feared that by doing so she would only attract men like the Governor, who would try to take advantage of her.

What she needed was a safe place to rest, where she could put her past behind her, hopefully for good. Judith looked to America with hope; maybe there she could recover the joy and peace she had once known at Shamash. Maybe there she could blossom again. Yet lingering in her thoughts was the nagging fear that she might be wrong – that America was like Persia, an illusion, decaying in corruption. Her only comfort came from believing that all this earthly unhappiness would pass someday, and if she remained steadfast and true to her God, she would be rewarded with eternal peace one day.

As the caravan crept along the barren mountain, travelers on horseback and in carriages formed a long thin line that slowly snaked up and around the mountain's edge. During the journey, Judith saw nothing that could distract her. The fertile plain and prosperous villages outside Hamadan had been left behind hours ago. There wasn't even a stray shepherd in sight. What lay ahead were grey boulders and snow-capped mountains. Contrasting with the jagged, grey stone masses piercing the sky was some sparse vegetation and trees that lent a touch of greenness to the monotonous setting. Beyond that, there was nothing, only her thoughts.

As her horse-driven carriage traveled into the unknown, Judith clung to the Queen of Sheba; it had become her intimate friend who, like Judith, had miraculously survived the war.

With this intimate friend she shared her most precious earthly gift, the brooch of Shamash, which she had pinned under the doll's dress. While snuggling close to her mother, chilled by the cool mountain air, Judith suddenly got it into her head to remove the brooch and stitch it inside the hem of her dress, as her parents had done with their gold. If she and her doll were ever parted again, at least she would still have her brooch.

As she hid the brooch in her hem, Judith thought about Kushi, and she wondered if she could ever be happy as his wife. He was safely in America, attending boarding school in Connecticut, removed from the cruel realities of the war. How would they respond to each other after what she had experienced? Would he still like her? She was no longer the innocent and ambitious girl that she had once been. There was no longer any yearning for world adventure. All she wanted to do was curl up somewhere and be alone. Would Kushi accept this? Or would he become just another expensive peacock with beautiful plumes roaming the world in search of pleasure?

Occasionally, she and her mother would exchange glances while riding over the narrow bumpy road, and Judith would wonder what Abigail was thinking. It was obvious by her mother's sadness that she too was troubled by their circumstances. Riding quietly along the mountain pass to Baghdad with Judith by her side, Abigail's sadness only lifted when Malko was near. At that moment, something sweet and beautiful occurred; a joy filled her, and she smiled radiantly.

To distract her temporarily, when they were alone, Judith engaged her mother in idle conversation. "How long will it be before we reach Baghdad?" she asked.

"Not long, my dear," her mother said without giving any serious thought to her answer.

"But we're still in the mountains. Baghdad is in Mesopotamia?"

"That's right, and Mesopotamia is just on the other side of the mountains. You'll know we're getting close when we start making a sharp descent."

Judith stared ahead at what seemed like an endless expanse of gray chunks of rugged mountains leading to snow-capped tips, when one of the wheels of the carriage slid over the mountain's edge. During that moment, when the carriage was dangerously close to overturning, she made the fatal error of looking down. Below she witnessed, to her horror, the cruelty of nature at work. A man's body was lying impaled on a boulder, and wild birds were tearing at his flesh.

She gasped.

Her mother put her arm around Judith, bringing her closer. "You mustn't look," she said to her daughter. "It will only upset you. Be brave, *ma petite*. We will be free soon."

Pained by what she had seen, Judith buried her face in her mother's sweater and held onto her tightly for comfort.

Her father rode alongside the carriage, when the road widened. Ever since he had recovered his gold, Malko had changed, becoming a new man, the invincible warrior he had always been. Judith wondered if money was the magic antidote for despair. If so, why wasn't her mother happy again?

Malko pointed toward a stream. "There's a clearing ahead. It should be large enough to accommodate the caravan. I'm going to tell the others to rest there for the night."

"Do you think we'll be safe here?" she asked.

"Yes, of course. Why would you ask?"

"I saw signs that there may be bandits on the road."

It was his turn to be comforting. "Don't you worry," he said confidently. "We'll be alright. We have enough guns and men to take care of ourselves."

"I hope so, Malko. I'm so weary of wars."

"It'll be over shortly, Abigail. We'll soon be in America, and this will all be history."

"Daddy," Judith interrupted, "are we very far from Baghdad?"

"Not far at all, Judith. We should be within easy reach of the British by tomorrow afternoon."

The clearing was a flat ledge against a soaring, snow-capped mountain peak. It was, as Malko had figured, sufficiently large to accommodate the entire caravan. A stream passed through a rock formation on one side of the mountain, and it flowed steadily across the clearing to the mountain's edge, where it disappeared. Malko and several of his men took the animals to the water to drink. The others raised the tents, filling the clearing with a multitude of portable homes. In no time, the lonely spot in the vast mountain range was filled with activity and became a gathering point where several hundred members of the caravan could socialize with friends and loved ones again.

"Where's Saul?" Malko asked while they were eating. "I haven't seen him for a while."

"His mule is probably acting up again," a man answered.

Malko smiled. "I told him he should have sold it and bought a horse. But no, he never listens. He's as stubborn as his mule. Maybe that's why they're so attached to each other."

While he ate and shared idle conversation with friends, a small group of travelers arrived. Worried they might be hostile, Malko quickly reached for his rifle, but he put it down when he saw a woman who sat on a donkey led by Saul.

Malko met them and introduced himself to the travelers.

"Where are you heading?" Malko asked.

"To Baghdad."

"Alone?" he asked, surprised.

"No, we were traveling by caravan before we were attacked. My husband and I were lucky enough to escape and find safety in a cave."

"Were those bodies along the road members of your caravan?"

"Yes," the woman said, visibly upset.

"Kurds?"

"I don't know. They weren't bandits, at least not ordinary bandits. All they wanted was information."

"What kind of information?"

"They said they were looking for a girl named Judith."

"Judith?" Malko asked, startled. "Judith Shamash?"

"Yes, that was her name, Judith Shamash."

"Do you remember the names of those men?"

"Only one."

"What was it?"

"Ejder."

Malko wrestled with the thought of sharing what he had learned with Abigail, but decided against it. It would serve no purpose. They must continue on their way and hope circumstances would permit them to reach the British safely before any harm could come to them. Once in the protective custody of the British, the family could put their fears behind them for good and make plans to secure passage to America. For now, he could only hope that nothing would interrupt their journey to Baghdad.

That evening, Malko set up a night watch. In the morning, he would send a small group of men ahead to patrol the road. Somewhere along this mountain trail, Ejder and his men were searching for his daughter. Malko suspected that the Governor had planned this search. His determination to locate Judith and claim her was threatening the safety of the entire caravan. Malko knew he couldn't allow his people to be massacred for the sake of his daughter. Yet on the other hand, he couldn't sacrifice his daughter to that criminal.

There was only one solution. He would have to think of a way of separating himself from the others to avoid bringing any further suffering on them. He must get those criminals to follow him, not the caravan. But how? Malko didn't know where Ejder and his men were. For all he knew, they could still be on the Persian side of the mountains, miles behind the caravan.

But when he gave thought to this, Malko knew it was unlikely. If the other caravan had recently been attacked by Ejder's gang, that would mean that the gang was ahead of them somewhere. Had the gang headed towards Hamadan, Malko would have collided with them during his journey up the mountain. This left him with only one question: *How far ahead could they be?*

Thinking about the possibility that Ejder might be near kept him awake that night. At dawn Malko was startled by the unexpected cry of a baby. At first, he gave little serious attention to it. He just assumed it was nothing more than a child calling for its mother. He was about to doze off, when he heard another unexpected noise - an audible gasp. It was followed by silence.

He looked to his left to see if Abigail and Judith were all right. He was relieved to note they were sleeping soundly; both mother and daughter were cuddled together warmly in the chilly morning air. He was about to return to sleep when he heard the sound of loose stones being crushed. This time he rose to his feet and looked outside. Men were entering the clearing; they were armed with rifles and sabers. The men were on foot, fanning out. Standing prominently among them, wearing a cape that was rippling in the wind, was Ejder. He was pointing in different directions, silently sending his men in small groups into key areas of the camp.

Malko immediately awakened his wife and daughter, covering their mouths with his hands to avoid having them make any sudden sound.

"You must hurry behind the rock formation by the stream," he whispered to Abigail.

"What's wrong, Malko? What's happening?"

"Now. Right away. There is no time to explain."

"But what about you? Aren't you going to join us?"

"I will," he said, "But first I must contact the others."

He watched his daughter and wife crawl away from the clearing and disappear behind the rocks. When he was sure they were safe, Malko grabbed his rifle and crept from tent to tent to alert the others one at a time. When he had notified as many as he could without being noticed, he rose up in the clearing and began to shoot. His first shot was aimed at Ejder, whom he wounded in the shoulder.

"Now it's your turn, *kuffar*," someone shouted from behind.

At the precise moment when Malko turned, a bullet flew past him, missing him. Before the man could shoot again, Malko shot and killed him. Other members of the caravan were rising from their tents and shooting.

As Malko's men surfaced, the remainder of Ejder's troops descended on horseback. Terrified women and children emerged from the tents, running in different directions. They were shot by the gunmen on horseback almost as soon as they surfaced.

Malko aimed his gun at Ejder once again, but before he could shoot, Malko was shot in the shoulder and dropped his rifle. Malko quickly removed his knife when someone leapt towards him. He plunged his knife into a man's stomach, and they both fell to the ground. Malko then shoved the dead man aside and was about to rise to his feet, when he saw Ejder standing above him, his saber pointed at Malko's throat.

"Give me your daughter," Ejder said, "and I'll spare your life."

"I don't know where she is."

Ejder pressed the steel saber against his throat. "Your daughter, Malko Shamash. Where is she?"

"She's in Hamadan with friends."

"Don't lie to me," Ejder said. He placed just enough pressure on the saber for it to sting. "I know she's here. Do I have to kill everyone to find her?"

"Why do you want her? What is she to you?"

A smile crossed Ejder's face, exposing his stained teeth. He seemed to derive enormous pleasure from what he was about to say. He was the conqueror with one foot on the chest of his victim. Hundreds of years of religious hatred were condensed in that one moment of triumph. "I have a buyer," he said contemptuously, "someone who has a fancy for Christian virgins."

His blatant contempt angered Malko. It was a savage anger, beyond anything Malko had ever remembered feeling towards anyone, and he grabbed Ejder's foot and lifted him and tossed him to the ground. Within moments, the two men were entangled, wrestling, each searching for some decisive way to eliminate the other. Malko grabbed his knife, which was lying nearby, and thrust it into Ejder's throat repeatedly until Ejder was lifeless.

Malko then grabbed a rifle and rose, but before he could aim it, he felt the pressure of a gun barrel against the back of his head. "Drop it, *kuffar*."

Just when he felt the gun against his head, he heard a familiar voice cry out loud and clear. "Don't shoot! That's my daddy."

Chapter 18

The British Hospital, Baghdad, Summer of 1915

Judith found it difficult to focus on what was happening around her. Whenever she tried to concentrate, her eyelids would involuntarily close. All she could see, when she forcefully lifted them, were blurred images distorted beyond recognition. Hovering over her, peeking through this blur, were two pairs of blue eyes.

"She's still bleeding, Doctor."

"Quickly," a man said. "To the operating room. We must stop the bleeding."

The anesthetic had taken control, leaving Judith too fatigued to think. Voices rose and fell around her, some more urgent and disturbing than others. They were the tearful voices of pain and sorrow. To the young girl on the gurney, being wheeled rapidly to the operating room, they were just meaningless sounds totally removed from her reality.

She awoke from the anesthesia hungry and confused with a violent headache. When she surveyed the room, she saw nothing familiar, nothing that would reveal exactly where she was. She turned her gaze inward. Perhaps she might uncover a clue in the dark labyrinth of her mind – a lingering fragment of reality that would lead her to discovery. But she was too tired to search. Her mind was a void, a *tabula rasa* with nothing, not even a fragmented image to examine.

A white curtain separated her from her neighbor to the left. The woman on the other side of the curtain was talking to someone. Her words were clouded with grief. Although the woman was able to control her emotion, some of it still spilled out as she spoke, interrupting her words with a whimper. The girl listened, feeling an undefined terror well up within her, as she was swept up in the woman's painful story. Each word the woman uttered brought the girl closer to the center of her own terror.

The pieces to her past fell together one by one. First there was the caravan, then the gunshot, and finally *the man*. All at once she was seized by a sorrow so disturbingly profound that her entire body began to convulse. The woman's story had opened the floodgates. With one inconsolable scream that seemed to last forever, Judith released her tortured pain for everyone to hear. Nurses rushed to her side in alarm.

A fourteen-year-old Christian Assyrian girl has been found alive after being shot at and left to die in the desert. Her name is Judith Shamash, born August 14, 1901, in Northwest Persia, in the village of Shamash. She is the daughter of Malko Shamash, a wealthy landowner, and his wife, the former Abigail Tamras, daughter of the prominent scholar and Presbyterian minister, the Reverend Daniel Tamras.

Anyone who recognizes the girl and knows the whereabouts of her immediate family should contact the British Hospital in Baghdad.

Judith tried to sort through her experiences and find some peace, some words of comfort to calm her. But all she uncovered in the dark corners of her past were mangled images of madness and hatred gone wild. Any comfortable memories of life prior to the war were obliterated by her painful recollections of decapitated and dismembered bodies. Every time she attempted to escape into some safe hiding place to forget, she would be yanked back into hell and placed on collision course with her past. When she thought she would never be able to find peace again, she remembered Psalms 27:1.

"The Lord is my light and my salvation; whom shall I fear? The Lord is the strength of my life; of whom shall I be afraid?"

By repeating the verse over and over again, Judith was able to absorb the full meaning of those words and tranquilize herself with the comfort of its message, which allowed her to fall asleep peacefully. This brief rest was unexpectedly interrupted by a hand brushing across her forehead.

Judith opened her eyes and to her surprise saw the Governor sitting beside her. He had with him flowers and sweets, which he placed next to her on the bed. When Judith looked into his blue eyes, surrounded by his abundance of well-maintained black curly hair, she saw worry. He no longer resembled the confident man he had once been. For several moments, she did not say anything. She was too surprised to see him, too frightened by his presence to respond. She just stared at him nervously. Old memories, which she couldn't suppress, returned.

"How did you find me?" she asked nervously.

"Your picture was in the paper."

"Why have you come?"

"I wanted to see you again."

"Didn't I make it clear I never wanted to see you?"

"Don't reject me, Judith, please. I want to marry you."

"That's impossible," she said. "My parents would never permit it."

"Have you forgotten? Your parents are gone. It's only you and me now."

She covered her face with her pillow to hide from the truth. With those pointed words, he reminded her what she was trying to forget. She was alone. No mother, no father, *no one* to protect her. She, Judith Shamash, was on her own at the age of fourteen. Any peace that she had found temporarily in the verse from the Psalms disappeared. This horrible monster who had brought her nothing but grief had returned to unsettle her again.

She removed the pillow and courageously looked her torturer in the eyes. "Go, please," she said. "I beg you. *Please* leave me."

"Don't hurt me, Judith, by rejecting me. Can't you find it in your heart to forgive me?"

"Forgive you? How could I for all the pain you caused me?"

"I know how much you've suffered. What has happened to you was horrible, but you are safe now. Let me protect you."

"Protect me? From whom? That crazy Kurd?"

"You need never worry about him. I took care of him personally."

"You…you…" She began, but she couldn't finish her thought. The words remained lodged in her throat. She didn't need for him to explain. She knew by just looking at him what he meant. She saw through him – as though he were transparent – to his corrupt core, which his handsome face could no longer hide.

"Yes, you're free, Judith. You'll never need to worry about him again."

She remembered the Kurd's violent act of domination and her struggle to survive in the dessert. She should've been relieved to learn that he was dead. But she wasn't.

"You didn't free me," she said bitterly. "How could you have freed me of him when he still lives in you?"

He pulled away from her, stunned by her response. When he recovered, his handsome face twisted into a demonic expression of hatred. "You refuse me? What conceit! You should be on your knees, thanking me for still wanting you. By marrying me, I offer you respectability again. Something no man will ever do after what that Kurd did to you."

"Get out of here, you horrid man. Get out of here before I scream my head off."

"Yes, I'll go, but I'll be back, Judith Shamash. The British won't be able to protect you forever. When I do return, you can be certain nothing will stop me from taking what I want, and *on my terms*."

She couldn't sleep, knowing that the Governor had found her. Of all the people in her life, why was he the only person who returned for her? Was he part of God's plan for her? She shuddered at the thought of submitting to him. *No, God could never be that cruel to me. It has to be a test. He is tempting me to see if I am strong enough to face what is ahead.*

Later that afternoon, Judith was wheeled into the courtyard, where she was able to relax in the sun. Lost in its warm embrace, she pushed aside any lingering thoughts she might have had of the Governor. She knew that as long as Baghdad was under British control, she had no reason to worry. Her thoughts lightened and her sad memories drifted away, partly because of the medication, and partly because of the pleasure the chirping birds splashing in the nearby fountain brought her.

Judith remembered Shamash, the Assyrian sun god, and the stories her daddy had told her about this great god of justice. She wondered if he were the same god that ruled America. Her granddaddy had told her many pleasant stories about America, how wonderful it had been during his student days at Brown College; similar stories had been repeated by other members of the family who had also studied there. "America was the only country in the world," her grandfather had said, "where freedom and justice coexisted, where a man could rise to the maximum level of his ability and enjoy the benefits of his labor." When she was better she would go there – after she found her parents – and discover this great land herself.

While relaxing in the hospital courtyard, observing the activities of nature, Judith saw a petite woman dressed in a nurse's uniform come towards her. She walked briskly in a no-nonsense, military way – shoulders back, chest forward, and head held high. There was only one person in the world she knew with a gait like that, and that was Auntie Suzy!

The sight of her awakened a joy that Judith hadn't felt for a long time. "Auntie Suzy," she said, throwing her arms around her.

"Darling, Judith," Suzy said. "What miracle of miracles! I found you at last."

She pulled a chair next to Judith, and she immediately began to fuss over her like a doting mother – fluffing her pillow, brushing a few fallen hairs away from her forehead, and straightening the collar of her hospital frock. Judith smiled contentedly, submitting with pleasure to the attention.

"How did you find me? Did you see my picture in the paper?"

"No, but I did see your name on the patients' list."

"Do you work here?"

"I have no choice. I have to, if I want to make enough money to get to America. The Brits aren't especially kind to us Assyrian refugees."

"They've been nice to me."

"They ought to. Look who you are." She began to fuss over Judith again, this time brushing away some of the crumbs from her dress that had fallen when Judith was eating a snack earlier. She then leaned back in her chair and smiled at Judith with affection. "Even in that unbecoming hospital frock, you still look like an Assyrian princess. They wouldn't dare be unkind to you. We are the Shamashes. Never forget that, my child! While the other Assyrians must live in camps like prisoners outside the city where they are denied sufficient food and water, we have been given comfort because of our family name."

"Why is that the case, Auntie? Aren't the British our friends?"

"We have no friends. Britain is like other European countries. It considers most of us savages. The British soldiers are here, not to protect us from the Kurds and the Turks, but because Britain wants the oil in Mosul and the Persian Gulf."

Judith began to shiver, as though the sun had disappeared and a freezing cold front had settled.

Baghdad was no longer as safe as she had believed. If the British placed more emphasis on the oil than on Assyrian lives, what would stop them from selling her off to the Governor for the right price?

"Is that what it's all about? Oil?"

"I'm afraid so," Auntie Suzy said. "No matter how well it's disguised, it's always about money, oil and land."

"What about my mamma and daddy? Do you think, if we gave the British enough money, they would find them for us?"

"I wish it was so simple, Judith. But no one knows what happened to them. When the camp was raided, most of the Assyrians were brutally killed. Some made it to Baghdad, while the others just disappeared."

Her tears began to flow – even the magic of medication couldn't hold back her grief anymore. "Do you think my mamma was stolen by one of those Kurds?"

"No one knows. You'll just have to leave it to the Lord and let time answer that question."

"I tried, *tantine*," Judith said. "But it's hard. Ever since I saw the Governor…"

Auntie Suzy pulled back, horrified. "You mean Sardar Jamshid?" Judith nodded. "Then that's who that is."

"Who?"

"The man outside in the carriage."

"Outside," Judith said. "You saw him outside?"

"Every day for the past few days, when I arrived at work in the morning and left in the evening, I saw him. He sat quietly in a carriage, observing the activity. I never thought it was him. Instead just a lookalike. But now, now that you've told me he was here, I am certain that is who it was."

Judith panicked at the thought of the Governor being so close, waiting for the right moment to claim her. "What'll I do?" Judith said, frightened. "He won't stop until he claims me. He told me that when he was here. How will I ever protect myself?"

"You will do nothing. You will just stay here and get better. I will figure out a solution myself."

"What about my mamma and daddy? How will I ever find them if he is always near?"

"Do you think if the British can't find them, you can?"

"But I must, " she said, tearfully. "I miss them so much."

"I know you do, darling," Suzy said, comforting her with a tender hug, which she sealed with a kiss on Judith's forehead. "I miss them too. But we will just have to be patient and let them find us."

"How will they ever know where to look for us, Auntie?"

"We will go to America as planned and wait for them at my brother's house. The Lord will do the rest."

"But what about the Governor? How will I ever get away from him?"

"Leave him to me. I'll think of something. But first I must figure out a way to raise money for our passage to America. The money Dakan sent me from America was stolen. Someone opened his letter and removed it. So that means I must work here until I save enough."

"I have the brooch Grandmamma left me. Will that help?"

"You mean the brooch of Shamash?"

"That's right."

Auntie Suzy threw her arms around Judith and squeezed her lovingly. "Will it help? *Of course it will help!*" she said joyfully. "That brooch is going to free us."

It was morning when Judith and Suzy decided to leave the hospital. Judith was dressed in white like a nurse, and the two women left the hospital with several other nurses whose shift had ended for the day. A carriage was standing near the hospital door, and Judith saw the man inside. She panicked at the sight of him. She wanted to break free from her aunt and run for safety into the hospital, but she was too smart to do anything so obvious and foolish.

"That's got to be the Governor in that carriage," she whispered to her aunt. "I can feel his cold blue eyes follow me."

"Lower your head."

"I'm afraid, *tantine*."

"Lower you head, Judith. He won't recognize you dressed as a nurse."

A man jumped from the carriage. "Judith?" the Governor unexpectedly called out. "Is that you, Judith? Please stop! I must talk to you."

"Run, Judith," her auntie said, pulling her rapidly down the street.

"I can't. It hurts too much when I try."

The Governor, who was quick and limber, grabbed Judith and pulled her towards him. At that same moment, her aunt released her hold of Judith.

"I told you I'd never let you go," the Governor said.

Her aunt hurried down the street, leaving Judith behind.

She betrayed me, Judith thought. *My own aunt betrayed me!*

"Auntie," she cried out.

"It's no use, Judith. Even your aunt doesn't want you anymore," he said. "No one wants you after what that Kurd did to you. I am not even sure why I still do."

"You're disgusting," she said bitterly. "I loathe you."

She was about to scream, alert everyone within hearing range of what was happening, but he quickly covered her mouth with his hands and pulled her close to him, as though they were family members reuniting affectionately. "No, my Judith. You aren't going to get away that easily this time. You are mine to enjoy, and nothing is going to stop me."

She began to kick and resist, in an effort to free herself, but he was too strong and too determined for her to succeed. He led her towards the carriage by the curb.

A British soldier appeared out of nowhere and yanked the Governor away from Judith. He then punched the Governor in the face.

Suzy appeared unexpectedly and grabbed Judith's hand. "Come Judith, we must hurry. We haven't much time to catch the boat. Don't worry about the Governor. I paid the soldier enough to hold him until we leave."

A carriage was waiting for them in the next block. In the carriage, there was another British soldier, whom Auntie Suzy had paid to escort them to the riverboat, which was docked on the Tigris.

"The boat to Basra leaves shortly," the soldier said. "We don't have much time."

When Judith and her aunt arrived at the port, the boatman was removing the gangplank. Suzy jumped from the carriage and halted him.

"Please," Suzy said. "We have to get on board."

"Impossible," the boatman said. "You'll just have to wait two days for the next boat south. This one is full."

"We can't wait that long," Suzy insisted. "It's a matter of life or death."

The thought of staying any longer in Baghdad with the Governor not far away terrified Judith. "We've got to leave," Judith said in tears to the boatman. "It's true. It *is* a matter of life or death."

Auntie Suzy discretely slipped a gold coin into the boatman's hand. He immediately smiled. "Hurry aboard," he said as the coin disappeared into his pocket. "I don't want anything to happen to you and your beautiful daughter." The two women quickly boarded.

As the riverboat paddled lazily south to Basra, where Suzy and Judith would board a freighter to Britain and then a steamship to America, Judith stared at the lifeless desert stretching beyond the banks of the river. She remembered the stories her father had told her about the mighty Assyrian Empire that had once ruled this uninhabitable area of the world until the Babylonians and the Medes destroyed it. Like the mighty empire that had once dominated Mesopotamia, everything from her past had been reduced to fine grains of sand. Nothing remained except a few dim memories of Shamash.

Tears came easily, involuntarily, sometimes even with a fit of emotion that reduced her to convulsive helplessness. Judith was a broken young lady who had lost her youth somewhere between Shamash and here without any graceful transition. She didn't know exactly when it began. Too many disturbing changes occurred too quickly to pinpoint the exact moment. As she watched the boat churn the water with its revolving rear paddles, she remembered the attack on their caravan.

One moment she and her mother were hiding at the edge of the clearing, watching in terror the brutal slaughtering of the Christians; the next moment Judith was running into the clearing where a gunman was aiming a rifle at her father's head.

"Don't shoot!" she cried out. "That's my daddy."

Unexpectedly, from nowhere, she heard a horse gallop towards her. A man grabbed her by the waist, lifted her onto his horse, and whisked her away down the mountain. Despite her tearful plea, her captor showed no sympathy. Alone in the desert with her, he was driven by a powerful lust.

Without consideration for her youth and inexperience, he took her roughly and cruelly, a hairy and sadistic beast who seemed to gain pleasure from her pain. Would she ever forget his insane and wild look that enflamed his desire? After he had generously enjoyed himself and Judith was lying there, in pain, unable to walk, bleeding, he spat on her, calling her foul names in Arabic before shooting her.

The details of this attack had come back to haunt her when she heard the woman in the next bed at the hospital tell her story. To calm Judith, the doctors had to dull the sharp edges of her memory with heavy drugs. But now, without medication, she could feel the pain again, as sharply as she had when the bullet entered her.

Each morning, during her long journey to America, when she dressed in front of the mirror, Judith would pause and stare at the ugly scar from her bullet wound, and she would remember that Kurd. Was this her punishment for daring to be a Christian in a Muslim world? Was the Governor right? Would her disgrace mean that Kushi and other decent men would reject her?

When she observed the other passengers on board the boat, she saw a reflection of her sorrow in their eyes. They too appeared to be people on the run, and like her, they were seeking a new life. She had no idea of what their unspeakable tragedy was, because no one was strong enough to mention it openly. But Judith knew each had their own heartbreaking story to tell. It was branded on them, as her scar was branded on her, and it revealed itself in their lifeless and sad expression.

As the steamship drifted slowly towards the New York harbor, Judith stood on the deck and stared ahead at the Statue of Liberty, which grew larger as the ship came closer to New York. This beautiful lady given to the Americans by the French had become a symbol of the only thing that mattered anymore to her. Would this be her new beginning? Would this tall and proud lady with a book in one hand and a torch in another be a symbol of the liberty she would soon know? She remembered the poem she had memorized in school.

"Give me your tired, your poor, your huddled masses yearning to breathe free," she said as the tears flowed. "I lift my lamp beside the golden door!"

Remembering, Judith too stood strong and tall with dignity. Through some miracle of faith, she was one of the lucky ones to make it to America's shore. Ahead, she faced a new life.

"*Je survivrai*," she said. "Thank you, dear Lord, for making it possible."

Epilogue

US Declares War on Germany

Los Angeles Herald Star (*April 6, 1917*) - Members of the United States Congress today declared war on Germany. The mounting pressure from the Americans, weary of President Woodrow Wilson's efforts to sidestep a military response against the Central Powers, ended this morning when Congress almost unanimously made the decision to fight alongside the Allies against the Central Powers.

Their decision to enter the war wasn't because of the sinking of the British passenger liner *Lusitana* by a German submarine, which drowned 1,200 people, including over 100 Americans; it wasn't because of Germany's policy to sabotage American ships carrying war materials to the Allies; it wasn't because of the Zimmermann Note, sent by Germany to the Mexican government, encouraging Mexico to declare war on the United States; and it wasn't because of Germany's continuous and indiscriminate submarine attacks against ships on international waters. It was instead because of all these things together, and one dramatic plea of a very vocal Assyrian teenager.

This teenager is Judith Shamash, and she lives with her uncle and aunt in the San Joaquin Valley. Her touching newspaper story about the atrocities committed against the Christians in the Middle East won her national attention and the complete sympathy of Congress.

"I beg you, Mr Wilson," she said during a national radio broadcast a few days after the publication of her story, "as the President of the greatest nation in the entire world, in the name of God and all things sacred, join forces with the Allies. The Central Powers must be defeated. They mustn't be allowed to spread their evil throughout the world. Maybe then others like me can live in peace with their mamma and daddy again."

Author

Joe David is the author of six books. His first book, *The Fire Within,* because of its successful dramatization of important issues in education, made the reading list at two universities and received national public attention. For about nine years, Mr. David was a frequent radio and television talk show guest in major U.S. cities, where he candidly discussed issues in education.

Over the years, he has written for professional journals, newspapers, magazines, and newsletters, including the Annenberg/CPB Math and Science Project, *Education, The Forum* (University of West Florida), *Hemispheres, Chile Pepper, U.S. Airways, Basic Education* (Council for Basic Education) and much more. His other books include *As Best We Can, Teacher of the Year, Glad You Asked!* and *Gourmet Getaways.*

CPSIA information can be obtained
at www.ICGtesting.com
Printed in the USA
BVHW04s0519120418
513156BV00005B/11/P

9 780939 360086

Joe David's latest book is in the great tradition of novels like Forty
Days of Musa Dagh *and histories like the* Rape of Nanking.
Editor George Thomas Kurian
The World Christian Encyclopedia (Oxford University Press, 2001)
The Nelson New Christian Dictionary (Thomas Nelson, 2002)

*In writing his novel, David not only demonstrates a significant
_____ oms and history of the times, but he also
_____ past in an exciting and meaningful way...
_____ impressive scholarship and memorable
characters.*

Anahit Khosroeva, PhD
Senior Researcher, Institute of History
National Academy of Sciences of Armenia

The Great War began with two shots: one aimed at the
Archduke Franz Ferdinand, heir to the Hapsburg throne
and the other aimed at his wife, Sophie. What many thought
would be just another Balkan squabble quickly escalated
into a major war felt around the world. As Europe burst
into flames and millions of soldiers began battling the forces
of nationalism, the Ottoman Turks joined arms with the
Germans and extended the conflict to their longtime enemies, the Russians and the Christians. Incited by secular
leaders in Constantinople, northwestern Persia became a
warzone in which radical religious tribes invaded Christian
villages and systematically martyred hundreds of thousands
of "infidels" who dared to resist conversion.

On a slice of ancient land owned by a wealthy Assyrian family,
a young Christian girl awakens to the brutal massacre of her
race in a war that she is too young to understand. Stripped of
her privileged and comfortable existence, pursued by a Muslim
governor — a symbol of the rising new world order — and
surrounded by hostility and greed, deep-seated hatred and
unspeakable horrors, she must somehow come to terms with
the nightmare that her life has become.

Books for All Times, Inc.
www.bfat.com

9 780939 360086